The Angel Chronicles Lucifer's Wrath

J.L. Rodriguez

The Angel Chronicles

Lucifer's Wrath

1

For my larger-than-life family, I love you all so much.

Love Always Prevails.

J.L. Rodriguez

The Angel Chronicles

Lucifer's Wrath

2

ISBN-13: 9781983249846

J.L. Rodriguez

The Angel Chronicles

Lucifer's Wrath

3

CONTENTS

J.L. Rodriguez

The Angel Chronicles

Lucifer's Wrath

4

J.L. Rodriguez

The Angel Chronicles

Lucifer's Wrath

6

"YOU SHOULD THANK ME FOR THE DEMONS IN THE DARKNESS. FOR WITHOUT THEM, WHO WOULD YOU BLAME FOR THE TRANSGRESSIONS OF MEN?"- LUCIFER

J.L. Rodriguez

PROLOGUE: A GLIMPSE

Maleki's large galactic eyes glazed over, in a trance as he focused on the flashes of visions in his mind, using his gift of foresight to find *her.* The others looked on in wait, a brilliant smile spread across his face when he saw her, she would ascend *tonight.* Jacey would be the first Healing Angel to ascend in over a hundred years and with her, they would now have two Healers in God's army.

Jesus knew this was a huge victory and it came not a second too soon. For the past century Lucifer had made it his personal vendetta to send his demonic influencers to corrupt the Children of Light. He stopped them from ascending by tainting them with evil. Although none of them were safe, his demons targeted the Healers as they were the most useful assets to Jesus.

Healing Angels could cure anyone injured and afflicted with the venom of evil and were priceless to have in battle. He desperately needed them to fight in the prophesied war against Lucifer's son, Damien and their massive demonic army. Which was why they'd gone through such extreme measures guarding Jacey insuring her ascension into God's army. With her, they would have a fighting chance at victory, sparing Heaven and Earth from Lucifer's wrath.

"Gideon, you must go *now."* Maleki ordered. "Your charge will need your protection while she ascends." He looked away and saw the danger she was in. "The darkness chases her! You must hurry, go!" Gideon nodded, "I'll bring her back." and closed his eyes to sync with his charge. When he felt her life-force, he created a portal and stepped through. He'd been watching Jacey for the past few years, protecting her from the darkness and demons since her Guardian had gone missing.

This was nothing new for many Angels had to step up and play double duty; replacing a Guardian who failed to return. No one knew how, or where they went, they just disappeared one by one until only God's Guardians remained. And *they* could not leave God's side, no, Jesus would never allow that, not in the condition his father was in. There was no question who was behind the Guardians going missing, it was Lucifer and everyone knew it.

Gideon came through the portal and stood shocked by what he saw. The darkness of the night didn't hide them, not from from his keen eyesight. Jacey was driving with a demon in her car, and three more on the roof. They clamored around jamming the brakes, taking control of the wheel and throwing her into a tailspin. He watched in utter horror as the small red vehicle flipped over, rolling down into a large ditch.

She was clinging to her life but Jacey wouldn't give up without a fight, she was stubborn and driven; he loved that about her. He rushed over to protect her attention and heard the low growls from the demons as they gathered around. It was his job to ensure her safety, to bring her back untainted, and he went into action to fulfill his duty.

One after another, he fought them off, but they kept coming back. *"They must want you something terrible."* He grunted as he threw a demon to the ground, piercing it with his sword. "Help! Please! Somebody!" Jacey pleaded. He could hear the fear and desperation in her voice and fought back every urge to help her; it was forbidden for a Guardian to reveal himself while a charge was still in their human form.

The demons swarmed, crouching around him like a pack of wolves readying to devour their prey. He smiled, twirling his massive sword in his hand. He would protect Jacey with his life, if they wanted her, they'd have to go through him first. "I need a good work out. Come and get me you ugly bastards! So I can send ya back to Hell in *pieces!"* They pounced, there were many of them, but they were uncoordinated and predictable. The fight was over within minutes. True to his word, Gideon had slain each one of Lucifer's pets.

He concealed his sword and stood by Jacey checking on her. She was nearing her ascension now, he could feel it, so he flew to the top of the ditch and waited, keeping a lookout for more demons. Although he knew it wouldn't be much longer, watching her suffer took an emotional toll on him. Gideon loved Jacey deeply and had for a while now.

There was something special about the way she carried herself. The tune from her life-force made him tingle whenever he plugged into it to find her. *She* was special. Smart, beautiful, hardworking and she was innocent; a rare attribute to have these days.

The transition would not be easy for her, although he wished it were. He knew what was in store for her as an Angel in God's army. She would have to train hard to become a formidable opponent, a warrior of God, and a Healer. Her success was necessary and the sake of Heaven and Earth rested on it.

Maleki and the other Watchers had seen Lucifer's plan and knew an attack on Heaven would happen. No one knew when or how it would all end, just that *he* was coming, and everyone, had to be ready for the fight of their lives... especially Jacey.

CHAPTER ONE: GOING HOME

A cold drop of rainwater hit my cheek, and I opened my eyes, screaming in agony, my lower body was trapped beneath the smoking wreckage of my car and I wondered what happened.

I couldn't remember the crash, but that didn't matter now, what mattered was that it was dark-- I was trapped in a ditch--no one would see if they drove by.

I tried to use my arms to wriggle free but the slightest movement caused excruciating pain. "Oh, God!" An agonizing cry slipped up my throat. But I wasn't a quitter --I refused to die like this-- I gritted my teeth, with the resolve I would free myself because my life depended on rescue, and I knew it. "Come on, you can do it!" I half shrieked, as if my command would somehow make me stronger. Giving one final push, with my last bit of strength, I muscled through the agony, in tears.

It was a wasted effort; I had made no progress and probably caused more damage to myself. "No!" I screamed as my arms betrayed my mind, they trembled and gave out--refusing to cooperate with my commands--and I collapsed back to the cold, wet ground exhausted and defeated. Well if I couldn't get out, maybe I could wait until morning where someone would surely see signs of a crash and come to investigate. I had to check my injuries to see if option two: waiting it out was a viable option.

Pain seared through my abdomen as I applied slight pressure with my hands, checking all of my organs and symptoms. *Pain in the abdomen, labored breathing, erratic pulse.* My heart sank with the realization that I was almost certainly suffering from internal bleeding.

As a third-year med student, I knew my prognosis; if I did not get help soon, I was going to die. There was nothing that could be used to draw attention to me with; I was surrounded by sticks and dirt the rain began to come down harder, drenching me beneath the cold wet night.

I cried out in pain, the wretched, broken cry of someone who was alone, in the middle of nowhere, and dying. My condition was deteriorating, the injuries too severe for my body to cope, shock would set in soon if it hadn't already, it wouldn't be much longer now..

"Help me! Please!" I screamed, shaking my head in frustration as I pounded the earth with my fists. Maybe I could fight the Earth itself, simply refuse to let her take me. Warm fluid filled my throat, I coughed, choking on the metallic taste of blood that swirled in my mouth. There was a desperate edge to my plea as I cried out almost in a whisper, "Please God, I don't want to die!!" I needed a miracle, and begged God not to take me.

Breathing was a struggle--and only getting harder-- I gasped getting less air each time while my heart pounded violently inside of my chest, the body's attempt to compensate for lack of oxygen. The end was coming, I could feel it. My eyelids were heavy, everything was fading into a dark blur when a bright light appeared. Adrenaline surged through my veins with the hope of rescue.

I lifted my head and saw a man walking towards me and smiled in sweet relief trying to focus on staying conscious. *Thank you God! Stay awake!* Stay alive! I commanded myself, refusing to give up.

There was an array of bright lights as he came closer, my eyes strained to focus. This can't be real... I could see him but something wasn't right; the light seemed to radiate off his body. It's a hallucination, an end-of-life hallucination. I remembered my studies on near-death experiences; they explain these delusions people create in their minds. Some claim to see a dead loved one, others have out-of-body experiences.

Refusing to fall a victim to my mind playing tricks on me, I squeezed my eyes shut and counted, one, two, three… When I opened them, I expected him to vanish—but that wasn't the case. He was still there and getting closer, I reached out to him, trying to signal I was alive.

The light was blinding now, I rested my arm on my face to shield my eyes from the intense rays that surrounded him. I couldn't speak, so I mouthed the word, "Please..." and my arm fell limp to the ground as I surrendered to the end.

The pain subsided and panic left my body, he reached out and held my hand just his presence was enough to reassure me. I'm not alone.

"It's all going to be fine" he said in a whisper, he had a beautiful thick Irish accent, I smiled, his voice was deep and strong yet kind. He brushed the hair out of my face. "I'm Gideon." Gideon... I smiled again. "I'm going to bring you home." He gripped my hand, pulling me up to my feet. A flash of light came and we were standing on the main road.

Whoa! What? Looking down at myself, I ran my hands along my body amazed that I stood there with no injuries. A laugh escaped me, I was so happy to be alive and looked at Gideon in shock.

"Thank you I — I can't thank you enough!" How is this even possible? "How—How did you do that?" He smiled, "I'll answer all of your questions Jacey— but first, we have to get you home." A jolt of fear shot through my stomach. *How does he know my name?*

He reached down grabbing my hand, I pulled it away and took a cautious step back. He glanced down and back up chuckling, raising his eyebrows. I stood a safe distance away and examined him.

His clothes were strange; he wore a long robe with a fancy gold clasp at the neck, it had two crossing swords in the center of a pair of wings. Beneath the robe, he wore a simple t-shirt, pants, and boots, all of it crisp solid white.

My breath caught as our eyes met, I'd been so lost in the miracle I hadn't really looked at his face before. He was beautiful in every sense of the word; the beauty that made it impossible to miss, tall with a strong, muscular build and a bone structure reminiscent of the Statue of David.

How can anyone look so different yet still perfect? His dirty blonde hair looked unkempt; hanging low, covering his ears and forehead in messy loose curls as if he were a couple months overdue for a trim.

His eyes held my attention, they were much larger than normal—but stunning and shined multiple shades of radiant blue with swirls of color that danced like water around his pupils. It was as if another universe existed inside of his exquisite irises.

He looked like he didn't belong here, he had human features yes, but something was still off about them. He shook his head, the movement drew me from the trance-like state I was staring at him in and I quickly averted my eyes.

"Well, we can't go anywhere if you don't trust me, Love." There was mild disappointment in his tone.

"Trust you? 'Love'?" I scoffed. "Listen Casanova, I don't even know who you are!" He laughed and placed a hand on his chest mocking offense. *That sounded rude... Whoever Gideon was, he saved my life, and I owed him at least a kind thank you before we parted ways.*

"Look, thank you for saving my life; I cannot even express my gratitude. But I'm just not comfortable holding hands with a stranger—and you are a stranger! Now, I can get home just fine by myself, I don't want to keep you held up any longer. So thanks again... God bless you and have a great night!" I patted him on the shoulder.

He looked like he was enjoying this; as if I were entertaining to him. *Is he crazy?* I gave him an annoyed look, but he held my gaze. *Is he just going to stare at me all night?*

His face grew serious, he cleared his throat and spoke. "Well no, we're not strangers to each other.... I told you my name is Gideon, I know your name is Jacey, and actually No, you can't make it home 'just fine by yourself' I told you I would take you home, which is what I intend to do so let's not waste anymore time Love...."

I didn't have time for this, it was already late, I turned and walked up the dark road, away from Gideon and his craziness. The sound of footsteps approached rapidly from behind and a pang of fear went through my chest. "Wait!" *AH! He's following me!*

I walked faster, until I was jogging, then full blown running, a hand grabbed my shoulder and turned around to tell him to leave me alone, "Leave—!" my face slammed into his chest, he grabbed my shoulders, forcing me to look at him.

Oh my God. He's a psycho! My eyes widened in fear while I thrashed back and forth screaming, "Let me go! Get away from me! Help!" Swinging my arms, trying to break free from his grip just caused him to hold me tighter—not enough to hurt me, but enough to keep there. Gideon was much larger than I was, I didn't have a chance of escape.

He tried reasoning with me. "Calm down Jacey! I'm not gonna hurt you! Would you calm down and just listen for a second — please!" He begged, his big blue eyes impossible to say 'no'.

This is useless. I let out an exasperated sigh. "What?!" not trying to mask my impatience anymore. He took a deep breath through his nose, as if *I* was the one annoying *him*, I scoffed. "I didn't come here to save your life Jacey, I came to bring you *home* Love—"

He looked at me, waiting for a response that wouldn't come. There were no words for what I felt. *Home…..* It echoed in my mind. "Jacey, I'm afraid your time is up Love." My chin quivered as I processed what that meant, my knees buckled and hit the ground.

My life…. is….. over? Everything inside of me shook, my heart broke as the realization of my death sucked the air out of me. *How? How could this be?* The darkness of the night that had just brought peace moments ago, now suffocated me with grief.

Gideon reached down, helping me to my feet. “Oh my God.” I cried, barely able to put one foot in front of the other as I dissected my final moments. *It all makes sense now; the pain went away... I died... It wasn’t a miracle.* My knees wobbled, forcing me to walk in a zombie-like state, I went back to the site of the crash and looked in the ditch and saw it: my lifeless body trapped halfway underneath my wrecked car.

I examined myself again running my hands numbly along my body. *What am I going to do? Am I going to be like this forever…. just existing? What happens now?* Gideon must know something.

I looked at Gideon, my eyes begging him for a comfort he could not give. His expression told me he understood, but could do nothing to help but there was a peace I found in Gideon's presence.

I had to say the words aloud to know what it felt like to acknowledge something so profound; the end of a human life— of my life—and the awareness of it. I’d have to accept it then. "I’m dead, my life—it’s gone." The words choked out in a stifled sob.

“Oh Jacey,” He gave me a cheerful smile and wrapped his arm around me. “On the contrary Love, you are more alive now than ever before.” His words made me hopeful. “There is still a lot that awaits you, but first—" He moved his hand in a circular motion, a portal of light formed, like magic.

This time when he reached for my hand, I accepted it with a smile. Gideon was never here to hurt me and I was no longer afraid. "Are you ready to see your new home?" I nodded, a sense of calm surrounded my body, and we took the first step in together.

The portal had bright streams of light and beautiful colors coming from all angles, drawing me in like gravity. When I stepped through the opening, I could hear the most magnificent music, soft and angelic chiming in my ears.

We were weightless and drifted in this other dimension as rays of colorful lights swirled around, lapping at my skin like heatless flames tickling everywhere they touched. My heart felt warmed with a love and peace I had never known before. Gideon guided me through the tunnel to another opening where we both popped out.

There was no question where I was when I saw the place; it had to be Heaven. We were standing atop an enormous evergreen mountain surrounded by every color you can think of. The sun was enormous and looked like it was burning with a glittering white and orange. The sky was a vivid array of purples, pinks, turquoise, white, orange and blues. As if God himself had painted it with radiant watercolors and throughout the white streaks, millions of stars shined like diamonds.

There were birds singing, flying through the waterfalls that roared from both sides. Above us, hundreds of colorful butterflies fed on the enormous flowers along every surface. This place was peaceful, untouched by man; natural, immaculate and glorious.

"Oh my God!" My hand flew over my mouth as if I had said a bad word as I whispered, "I'm sorry!" and looked around paranoid I was in trouble.

Gideon burst out laughing, "Relax Love! He doesn't care about that!"

I let out a relieved sigh. "So, I take it you will not stop calling me 'Love' anytime, huh?"

"Ah, It's just the way I talk Love, I mean no offense."

I smiled and shrugged, it was growing on me anyway, just like this place. There was boundless beauty of unimaginable proportions and utter happiness within me, I was in a state of euphoria. Taking a deep breath, I opened my eyes, embracing my new life. *So this is home— I'm home.*

CHAPTER TWO: WINGS

Gideon blew his breath out and slapped his legs. "Well, there's no time like the present, how about a tour and a few introductions? There's a lot more coming your way!" He motioned for me to follow and walked down a narrow winding path that went under a canopy of bright pink, violet, and blue flowering trees.

It was hard not to be captivated by the beauty surrounding me, I had to force myself to keep up, all I wanted to do was stand still and memorize every single detail of Heaven.

Please don't let this be a dream. I want this— I need this to be real. I laughed at the irony of my thoughts. *One second, I'm begging not to die, and the next I'm hoping I did. Crazy much?* I felt like this place just couldn't exist; it was too perfect. On earth if something was too perfect, it's almost always fake. I wrestled with the idea that this... experience was no exception to that rule. *You know what they say? If it's too good to be true, it is….*

"There is so much for you here Jacey." Gideon said, pulling me out of my thoughts. "We have been waiting for you for — an eternity!" He laughed like he had just told a joke.

"I don't get it." and shrugged my shoulders.

"A little heavenly humor." he explained. "You know because we are here for an eternity—" He rolled his hand towards me with the punch line and dismissed the thought. "It's funny—you'll get it later." he chuckled again.

I smiled and nodded, appreciating the effort he was putting into helping me. I needed someone to talk to and help me work through this whole ordeal. My mind and senses were in overdrive, I had some adjusting to do, my life had literally flipped upside down in the blink of an eye.

There were a lot things I didn't know and so many questions, hopefully, Gideon would have the answers to. "So…." I reached my hands above my head, touching the soft petals of the flowers as I collected my thoughts. "Can I ask you a few questions?"

"Please do. Consider me your tour guide, and personal advisor, M'lady." he opened his arms motioning throughout the length of his body, "I'm at your disposal love, ask away."

I fidgeted with my hands and bit my lip, a million questions roamed around my head. *He said 'ask away'...*"Why don't I have wings? Why don't *you have wings?* Are you an Angel? Am I? Why are we walking can't we fly? Does everyone become an Angel when they die, or is that just in movies? Where is God and Jesus? Don't they like, stand you before them and judge whether you are worthy to come to Heaven—"

Gideon put his hands up for me to stop. "Okay,—slow down there Love. Let's take it one question at a time shall we?" I nodded, embarrassed. "All right let's see, well first, yes, I have wings and you do too, at least—you *will*," He was keeping track of each question he answered with a count of his fingers. "Second, flying is the preferred mode of transport here, we can *all* fly, third, yes, I am an Angel and you are too, but we are not the Angel you're thinking of flying in clouds playing harps and stuff." He fluttered his hands dramatically.

"I am a Warrior Angel in God's army, but *you* are special because you are a Healing Angel" I raised my eyebrows, shocked and he nodded at me. "It is one of the highest honors in God's army and you're the *rarest* you have no idea how long we've been waiting for you." *I'm what?*

"That's not possible... there's——there's no —— there is no way." I stammered. It made little sense for me to be an Angel, let alone one in 'God's Army' I was just a normal girl — who led a regular life, almost boring in fact, so how could I be qualified for any army?

Gideon raised his eyebrows and tilted his head. "Oh, It's possible because it's what you were *created* for—" He continued counting with his fingers picking up where he had left off answering all of my questions. "Fourth, no, not everyone that dies gets to become an Angel, you must be chosen— created with a gift, for a purpose." He was talking with his hands as he explained, his face full of passion.

"And as far as God and Jesus…. God, is the almighty. You were judged before *I* ever came to bring you here. He manages the entire universe from a higher level of Heaven we don't see him often, don't worry though, he is here, everywhere all around just as he is on Earth. Now Jesus—He is *our* leader."

He pointed his fingers between us "I'm *trying* to take you to him and introduce you so *he* can explain everything else—and there's a lot more to explain trust me. But listen Love, we'll take forever if we keep stopping to talk like this— not that I don't enjoy it." He finished with a wide grin and a wink that could melt every woman's heart on Earth.

Chagrin filled me as I caught myself staring at him admiring his perfection with a big dumb smile on my face. *Ugh! I should NOT be staring at him like that!* I looked away, I would have flushed bright red if I were still alive, and thanked God that I wasn't.

He'd answered my questions, but that did nothing to resolve them for me. *What does a Healing Angel mean? 'God's Army?' Jesus is our leader?* My face lit up with the realization I was en route to meet Jesus face-to-face.

"Let's go, I want to meet Jesus!" I raced down the trail, excitement flowed through my body. Gideon pulled my arm, spinning me around on my toes.

"Whoa, wait a sec! As much as I enjoy stretching my legs and giving you the grand tour on foot—If you want to get somewhere fast, I think you'll appreciate the efficiency of our preferred mode of transport—" He grinned, "You *seemed* interested in flying, after all."

I put my finger up to speak, and opened my mouth but closed it as I watched Gideon take a deep breath and bend forward. A gold and white orb circled between his shoulder blades giving life to a pair of glorious wings.

Gideon's wings were breathtaking and huge; at least 12 feet across. They had gigantic lustrous white feathers tipped with Gold and shined as if each quill was composed of diamonds. He held his arms wide open, spinning in a circle to show them off. "Well? What do you think of these? Want to give her a go?" I nodded with my mouth still gaped open.

He's beautiful. Every part of him was pure perfection, I blinked, swallowing hard and shook my head trying to concentrate and form an intelligent sentence with little success. "Um—yes! H-how did you—how—do I do it? H—how do I make them—um—come out of me?" I ran my hands through my hair.

Wow. That was a fail. I turned my neck and leaned my shoulder forward to check and see if there was any sign of wings but there was nothing. "How do I get my wings?"

"Okay, so think of this place as an 'anything is possible' place... anything you could want or imagine." I couldn't think an 'anything is possible' place could exist... even in Heaven.

"We have this energy and power to create within us, it's called life-force. We share this life-force with God and each other.

It's a connection, and once you tap into it BAM! Anything is possible! So first, close your eyes—" He coached and stood behind me placing his hand on my back where my wings would be, I felt a static shock like tingle where he touched, giving me goosebumps, and tried to ignore the sensation, concentrating on his voice.

"Try to imagine what your wings look like. Picture every single detail— anything you want, draw your wings in your mind and imagine them forming onto your body. Just relax, and feel your life-force, feel your energy, God's energy, my energy—we're all connected" He placed his hand on my chest over my heart and I could feel the heat radiate between us, I took a deep breath. *Get yourself under control.*

"It rests in your chest where your heart was when you were human." *Okay, that makes sense.* "Find it and use your power to *bring them to life.*"

Closing my eyes as instructed, I felt a warm humming in my chest and smiled. *I found it... my life-force!* Once I connected to it, my entire body was humming, and I focused the energy picturing myself with glorious white and emerald tipped wings. They had silver stripes and black diamond quills and glistened in the light, I imagined the energy orb I saw coming out of Gideon and directed it to come out of me, forming my wings.

When I opened my eyes, I turned to look at my back and saw them: my wings. A delighted shriek came out of me. "Whoa!" They were more beautiful in reality, I dipped my shoulder forward to get a better look giving them a little flap. They felt like a part of me; no different from a hand or an arm. "They're amazing! Magnificent!" Flapping my wings until my feet lifted off the ground.

"Oh now see, you—you were made for this! Your wings are perfect! They suit you well, gorgeous!" He stood staring at me, I beamed, not minding the extra attention from him and glad he seemed so impressed.

"Let's give them a test drive!" I laughed but stopped as I realized he was serious.

He wanted to fly… and he wanted to do it now. *Great. Now I get to die, again.* With all that talk about wings and flying, I had somehow failed to mention I was afraid of heights. *Great.*

CHAPTER THREE: LOVE AT FIRST FLIGHT

Flying, as fun as it sounded to most people without phobias, terrified me to the bones. *Okay. So I'm gonna fly.* I contemplated the possibilities, trying to gain the nerve to overcome my fear. *What if I can't stay in the air?* Although, I was already dead, the innate self preservation instinct lingered leaving a sick feeling in the pit of my stomach. Flying was unnatural; humans don't fly, and I definitely classified it as an activity that *could* cause my demise.

I sucked in a sharp breath and tried to keep a casual tone. *Play it cool...* "So, um-what do we have to do to—you know," Pointing my finger towards the pink streaked sky, "get lift-off?"

"Just watch me first— don't be nervous, you'll see once you get up there, it's *easy and so much fun!*" He bent his knees, looked up, and shot into the sky. I watched for a minute. *He looks like he's enjoying himself.*

He was whooping with laughter and flipping around, giving me a little show. His remarkable display enticed me; I wanted to join in on the fun. I decided to give myself a little pep talk before committing to the act. *"I got this. No big deal. You can do this."* I was borderline hyperventilating, pacing back and forth.

"Are you coming? Or are you gonna stand down there talking to yourself all day?" he teased, hovering above my head.

"Oh, I'm coming!" I snapped back, feigning irritation. *Well, here goes.* With a deep breath, I bent my knees, looked up to where Gideon was, and pushed with all my might off the ground.

I zipped past Gideon like a bullet with no sign of slowing down. "Whoa!" and flailed my arms trying to balance myself, panicked I yelled, "Gideon! Do something! How do I STOP?!"

He was on my heels, "Just open your wings wide and push the air up—" He shouted up, at this point he was holding his stomach from laughing so hard, "Stop trying to fly with your *arms* Jacey! Use your wings!" He was in hysterics at my less-than-graceful performance but I had no time to feel ashamed.

Oh. I hadn't even realized my wings were closed, tucked to my back. *Excellent for take-off, but terrible for active flight.* I thought. *Well, this should help. M*y wings opened as wide as I could and I halted, panting with relief. A sense of pride filled me as I realized I had faced my fear and overcome it.

"Hey, this isn't so bad!" *I'm getting the hang of this.* I got the feel of flying, flapping my wings as I gauged their power and practiced balance and control.

As soon as I figured that part out, I found that flying was like breathing; effortless, my body just did it. My wings supported me and felt powerful and strong. I was high on the joy of flying, in love with the freeing sensation it brought.

"C'mon!" Gideon flew in front of me, with his back facing the ground and hands resting behind his head, he looked like he was reclining mid-air. "Show off." I teased. "Okay, well, let's see what *you* can do!" he flipped through the air spiraling down, then up again.

"You know, we Angels can do anything!" He yelled at the top of his lungs and disappeared high into the fluffy clouds above us. *All right, let's do this.* I pumped my wings with all my might, determined to keep increasing my speed until everything I passed became a blur.

It's kind of like swimming. Dry swimming, I feel weightless. I flipped forward in the air and plunged myself in a straight dive towards the ground and popped my wings open wide like a parachute to stop. Then I thrusted them down shooting myself back up again. Now, I was right behind Gideon whooping with joy I snagged his foot. "Ha! I got you!" He looked back at me and grinned.

"Took you long enough, slowpoke!" Gideon teased as I pushed as hard as I could to fly a nose ahead of him.

"Slow-poke? Just wait until I get the hang of these bad boys," I retorted back as I motioned to to my wings, "you'll be eating my Angel dust then!"

He chuckled dipping his shoulder into mine. "We'll see about that! You let me know whenever you're ready — I got nothing but time." He gave me that disarming smile and a wink.

I looked away grinning like a schoolgirl and realized at that moment I had a serious crush on Gideon. *I have got to get a grip…. Angels probably aren't even allowed to date.* The thought itself unsettled me.

In all of my twenty-four years on earth, I had found no one as attractive as Gideon. Not just by his looks, everything about him seemed perfect for me. His voice, his demeanor, personality, and kindness… there was *something special* about Gideon that spoke to my soul. I never wanted him to leave and I had only just met him.

I wondered if I was experiencing some psychological infatuation with Gideon because he was the one who saved me. *I'm feeling this way as a part of my psyche trying to handle the magnitude of change I went through.* I mulled over the idea for a moment feeling more like my rational self. I needed to excuse the intense pull I felt towards him, and I felt it. *He makes me feel peaceful and safe that what's so attractive about him, I'm in a new place and uncertain and Gideon makes it better, that's all. This is ridiculous.* I thought to myself *I'm crazily infatuated with an Angel whom I just met.*

I wanted to feel normal... these feelings, this intense attraction was *not real* I reassured myself and pushed the critical thoughts to the back of my head. I looked around trying to find a distraction for my mind, luckily Heaven offered an abundance. The sky, the colored terrain, this place was out of this world.

Gideon pointed to a clearing between the clouds, "Do you see that field over there?" I followed his finger to an enormous field surrounded by trees and mountains. There were Angels down there, split into several large groups. *What are they doing? Why are they fighting one another?* "Yes— but why are they fighting?"

"They're not fighting, they're *training, love!* C'mon, there's someone you've been dying to meet!" he grabbed my hand, and we swooped down towards the field.

CHAPTER FOUR: A WARM WELCOME

Confusion filled me by what Gideon had said about the Angels training. *Why would Angels need to train? What happened the promise of an 'eternity of peace' in Heaven?* When we landed, all the Angels stopped what they were doing and rushed towards us. There were dozens of beautiful faces surrounding us in an instant, coming for hugs and hello's. I had never felt such kindness, from strangers.

"Gideon, my friend!" I heard someone shout, "So glad to see you have made it back!" A male Angel stepped forward out of the group with his arms stretched wide embracing Gideon. *Who is that?* There was something familiar about him. I couldn't quite place it, but I *felt* like I knew him from somewhere. He was the biggest of all the Angels; standing almost a foot taller than Gideon. He had long, dark, wavy hair with tan skin, and the most vivid large turquoise green eyes I had ever seen. But it was his voice that captivated me most. *I know that voice from somewhere.*

I didn't even realize I was staring at him until Gideon turned. He was embracing his friend, "Jacey, I believe this—" he pointed to him. "—is who you were asking for." My jaw dropped, and I put my hand to my mouth as I realized who it was, tears streamed down my face. “Jesus.” I breathed in a whisper that was barely audible. “JESUS!” I screamed and jumped into his open arms, squeezing him with all of my heart. *This is the best hug I've ever gotten in my life!*

“Welcome, Jacey” Jesus said in a comforting tone as I wept into his chest. He hugged me and patted my back like a father comforting his daughter. “I am so glad you're here with us—you're home now!” He smiled as he pulled my shoulders back to look at my face.

“Thank you! I'm SO HAPPY!” I couldn't stop smiling as I dried my tears. He nodded at me, with such love in his eyes it almost made me cry again. “I know you have many questions,” Jesus began, “and I promise you'll find that in Heaven, there is ample time to answer every single one of them” he shook his head laughing along with all the other Angels.

“Angels, let's take a break from training for the day so we may welcome Jacey with open arms and show her the beauty of her new home!” he placed his arm around my shoulders and raised his fist in the air.

“Tonight, we celebrate Jacey!”

“YEAH!” all the Angels shouted. I scanned the crowd looking for Gideon who had somehow disappeared while I was speaking with Jesus. “I'm right here.” Relief washed over me the moment our eyes met, I felt more grounded when Gideon was near, he was something tangible and real.

"Everyone, go home, and change out of your training clothes. We will meet at the Hall tonight." Jesus finished, as all the Angels came up saying goodbye as they passed before flying away to their homes. There were so many faces each Angel unique just as each person is.

Wow. It will be impossible to remember everyone's names and faces. Good thing I have an eternity to figure it out! I laughed out loud and nodded to myself. *Yep. I get it.* Chuckled again. *Nothing but time.*

"Are you ready to see your new home?" Jesus asked. "Yes, I'm ready!" I was feeling like a kid on Christmas; everything was a gift and exciting. I wondered if this feeling of euphoria was permanent—enjoying living at the moment like this. "Follow me!" Jesus yelled as he shot up and out of the field. "C'mon" Gideon grabbed my hand, and we both followed, "Where does everyone live at?" I asked, curious as to what the typical living arrangement was in Heaven.

there Angel suburbs?Is it a city of Angels? Or an apartment building? An Angel bee hive? Imagining everything I could and coming up with no answer that seemed to fit. "You'll see" Gideon said sharing a sly smile with Jesus.

"Heaven is not like earth, and Angels are not like people," Jesus began, "We are people in appearance, but we are not earthly people, we are—" he paused looking for the right words.

"Think of us as being on another level of existence. We are people, we all lived, and died on earth—mostly, but we don't get tired, or thirst or hunger. We don't get sick by any normal means — but it feels *good* to drink, and eat, and sleep." *Interesting. No wonder I haven't felt the least bit tired, just strong and full of energy.*

"It's more of a human habit than anything else." Gideon added, "When I first got here, it felt so weird never being tired, or hungry; I slept and ate all the time just out of the desire to hang on to my humanity."

Jesus burst out in laughter, "What do you mean you 'ate all the time'? Every opportunity you have you're eating still! It's a good thing we can't gain weight otherwise you'd be a very chubby Angel— incapable of battle!" He tapped Gideons stomach.

"I'll show you incapable!" Gideon laughed diving at Jesus. They rolled around in the air wrestling one another like brothers. I watched and laughed at their boisterous display of boyish fun with a smile; they were adorable. After a moment, they collected themselves and joined me on either side again.

"What I'm *trying* to say," Gideon continued, "Is that it is unnecessary for our survival anymore." We grew quiet and looked ahead where the clouds were breaking.

Jesus' face lit up as the sun hit it, its rays reflected off of his turquoise eyes making them shine. "You will find your own way to enjoy eternity Jacey, we want the world for you, all of your heart's desires—starting with this."

My breath caught as I saw where we were. There was a small section of beach where the sunset glistened off the water and radiated all the colors of the rainbow. No one could know what that beach meant. Well, only God and, Jesus.

CHAPTER FIVE: DREAM HOUSE

I stepped onto the empty white beach. It was a beautiful sight, the sultry smell of salt water radiated off the shore, the powdered sugar feel of the sand beneath my feet, and the rainbow colored facets that seemed to be a part of the water as it reflected the colorful sun was breathtaking. But there was no house; I saw nothing except the horizon and sand. "Where's the house?"

Gideon smiled, "Well, if I had to guess where it would be—" he held his hands in a square as if he were making a frame and looked at me, "I would say you're standing on it." I looked down at my feet like the ditz that I was and then back up to him incredulously.

"There isn't anything here." I said still half expecting my feet to rumble beneath me as a house magically appeared—it was Heaven after all—I could count nothing impossible after what I've witnessed.

Jesus came up beside me and placed his arm over my shoulders. "Not yet," he patted my back. "But there will be — your home works much like everything else here in Heaven." He tapped his temple, his turquoise eyes reflecting the water behind me. "The only limitation is in your mind. Nothing comes to be until you create it."

Interesting, magic—that's what I figured. "Remember when I showed you how to make your wings?" Gideon asked, "Yes." I flapped my wings happy to have another opportunity to show them off.

"Well, *everything* works like that here. I told you: you can have *anything*—your very own happy place. Just use your life-force to create it." He held his hand open and hundreds of tiny golden orbs circled, leaving behind a single rose. "See? This for you, Love." He handed it over, I accepted, smelling the light floral aroma and trying to ignore the electric shock that seemed to pulse through me every time Gideon was near.

"You have so much more to learn here Jacey—Heaven is a place of magic and happiness—anything is possible here. You deserve this home to be exactly what *you* want. After all, you *are spending eternity here.* What better way than to make it yourself? To truly understand that you can make your dreams come true..." Jesus said, encouraging me.

I examined the rose—twirling it in my fingers by its stem—every detail was perfect. Gideon just materialized it from thin air. I can do this. Details... I know what I want. It will be perfect. After a long relaxing breath, I centered my energy releasing the air. The energy was surging through me, felt my power, felt the life-force running in my veins and pulsing from my chest like blood, like a heartbeat. If I would create a home out of thin air while Jesus and Gideon looked on at the magic of my thoughts, I wanted to do it right, so I settled in and ignored my audience. I could try—I would try—to make my dream house a reality.

I moved my feet, driving them deeper into the powdery white sand and stared into the sunset thinking about my past. It all seemed so distant now, almost as if this was my life all along and my humanity and mortality was nothing more than a dream. It was strange because I did not mourn the life I may have missed on earth—maybe God had done me a kindness—I felt no sadness. Did I feel nervous? Absolutely. But Sadness or pain? No, there was no room for those feelings—almost as if they didn't exist—and I was grateful for that. Being an Angel and spending eternity in Heaven felt so right, so magical, I wouldn't wish for anything else; I'd found my happy place.

I could smell the salt in the air and it relaxed me and focused my thoughts. I closed my eyes and imagined me standing in front of my home. It was a white beach house with blue shutters and a wrap-around porch that had a sun bleached dock that led all the way down to the water.

Inside, my home was all white; couches, bedding and carpets with the occasional teal and chocolate brown décor to add a splash of color. In my windows were sheer white curtains that would billow as the midnight breeze rushed in from the ocean. I had a bed with a driftwood frame and rustic charm. There was wicker patio furniture—it had teal and pink floral patterns on the cushions—just like my grandmother had when I was a child. I imagined every detail of my home as best I could.

That's everything, let's see if this actually worked or if I've just been standing here like an idiot with my eyes closed for the past ten minutes. When I opened my eyes to see my new home a mere four feet away from me, just as I had envisioned.My mouth dropped open with an audible pop and I scrambled around in my head to remember how to speak. My eyes were stinging, tears threatening to spill over—I wiped them away—as I stood in awe of my creation. "Welcome home Jacey!" Jesus and Gideon exclaimed, throwing both hands in the air with enthusiasm.

"We have much more to do," Jesus spoke, all business now "And there's a lot to discuss, with many more introductions to make, I must go prepare for our celebration!" He looked over at Gideon, who nodded and then looked back. "Gideon will stay with you to help you adjust and become comfortable finding your way around Heaven. Consider him your chaperone for the foreseeable future. He will also be your trainer when the time comes. If you need anything, give me a shout; I'm always around!" I didn't think I'd ever get used to speaking with Jesus—my mind stuttered to a stop whenever I saw him—it was just surreal. And before I could process what he'd just said and say 'goodbye'—he was gone.

We stood in front of my new home in silence for a moment lost in the magic of this place. To have everything I could imagine seemed so far fetched and unrealistic where I came from. Yet, that was my new reality; a world without limit.

"So, are you going to show me your new home?" he said, his tone light "Or are we going to stand out here *forever*?" He rolled his eyes with an emphasis on the last word and I giggled, finally understanding the punch-line to his eternity joke earlier. There is no concept of time here, no time to sleep, eat, go to work, no clocks, no payday, or bills. It was all different here and the striking concept of humans always being rushed for time was comical when eternity was in play.

What was the need of clocks and timekeeping if we did not age or have earthly needs and obligations? I had spent all of my years on Earth grinding towards a life that was never meant to be—I was meant to be an Angel—and being an Angel was growing on me. I jumped up the stairs beaming as I stood beside my open door bowing to show him through the entrance. Using my absolute fanciest butler voice, I bowed, rolling my hand,"Welcome, to my humble abode." Gideon laughed at my performance—the beautiful sound was almost musical, it made tingle—and I chastised myself mentally for crushing on him so bad as we stepped into my dream house.

CHAPTER SIX: GUEST OF HONOR

Being inside the reality of my thoughts was a unique and deeply personal experience—it was hard to remember that this was real—I ran my fingers along every surface to make sure it was. *It feels real.* "Wow, Jacey—" Gideon gushed in awe as he looked around. "Thanks—I used to dream about a home like this when I was younger—although I never expected to get it in this manner." I laughed a nervous laugh as he walked through the living room to the French doors leading out onto the back patio. I wondered what he was thinking—his eyes were careful, almost nervous—as he leaned over the banister.

"You have good taste." He smiled looking out onto the beach. I smiled back, appraising his light curls in the sun, letting my eyes wander down to his muscular arms and chest, his large hands and sighed dreamily. Yes, I suppose I did have good taste good taste in homes and I certainly had good taste in gorgeous Angel men—dammit—why did my mind always wander back to these thoughts? And why was he so beautiful anyway? No one has to be *that* devastating to look at it's— unfair actually—and it could be dangerous.

He pressed his mouth together fighting a smile that played around the edges and stifled a laugh, "What's so funny?" I asked? He just looked at me smiling and shaking his head, his blue eyes smoldering, "Nothing Love, something funny just popped into my head." He locked eyes with me again and I forgot the question as we shared the intimate gaze, I was on cloud nine and for the moment, oblivious to my previous quest for answers and clarity. A part of me still felt like I *needed* to know everything about Heaven and Angels. I realized being an Angel meant more than spending endless days inside of a luxurious beach house.

I know that Gideon's a Warrior Angel... the name itself implies that there must have been or will be.... a war. What I didn't know however, was what *my* role in all of this was. What could I possibly have to offer? The ignorance unsettled me. There was still a lot I didn't know, and I had no choice but to wait until they told me everything.

I stood beside Gideon looking at the ocean, listening to the gentle lapping of the waves against the sand, a million questions running through my mind. I wonder what they will discuss with me tonight. Why would they celebrate my arrival? What did Gideon call me again—A *Healing Angel*—what's my purpose here as far as *that goes?*

Gideon spoke with soft wisdom in his voice, "I know you still have a lot of questions Jacey. I promise you will know everything soon." He walked back inside, I followed him over to the bookcase as he perused through my favorite novels—walking across them with his fingers—until he found one he liked. "Again, excellent taste." I laughed lightly, "Thank you, I've always been an avid reader. Books are—were—kind of my thing." He gave me a half smile then placed the book back on the shelf and cleared his throat. "Why don't you go get ready and I will be back to get you for the dinner?"

With no idea of what I should wear, I looked down at my clothes and back up to Gideon, embarrassed. *Still wearing the clothes I died in... that's attractive.* "What should I wear?" I asked. He laughed, "Don't worry we make it easy for you here. Every Angel has several particular items to wear that never change." He walked into my bedroom and opened my closet, "Go on, have a look for yourself."

There were 3 items hanging in my large mirrored walk-in closet. One was a long white gown with sleeves and an open back they designed with space for our wings, another outfit was a two-piece set, it had thicker material, more durable with long sleeves, and pants; it was white and silver—it would fit well to the body—it matched what the Angels in the field were wearing earlier.

The third item hanging was a thick white robe like Gideon was wearing, except for the Gold clasp at the neck of mine had a cross in the center of a pair of wings. "You should try this—" he said holding the elegant gown out gingerly to me. I gave him a skeptical look. I wasn't a 'dress' type person—never had been—I preferred comfort and had practically lived in scrubs throughout my adult life. He shrugged his shoulders and hung my gown back up walking back toward the door.

"It's up to you, I'll give you your privacy." He winked, a bright smile on his perfect face that would have made me blush if such a thing were possible, "I'll be back soon." My stomach knotted at the realization that I would be alone, for the first time as soon as he left. I called out to him, not knowing what I would say yet—or why I wanted to say something—to make him stay even a second longer.

"Wait!" he turned to face me, his eyebrows raised, "Yes? Did you need something else Love?" He searched my face, trying to read my expression, his penetrating stare made me feel strangely exposed, vulnerable even. I struggled to find the words. "I—well um—I just wanted to—" I sighed, maybe I was going crazy what do I say? 'I don't want you to leave me? Privacy be damned—I can't imagine a second without you—that doesn't sound obsessed and psychotic at all. I shook my head and breathed, resigning to the fact that clearly I was insane and I had to let him go—I would be fine—he would be back soon. "Thank you Gideon—for everything—you've made this whole transition so much easier, and I appreciate it." I settled it at that, deciding to keep my insanity to myself.

He tipped his head. "That's what I'm here for Love, you don't have to thank me—I'm happy to do it." He turned to leave yelling over his shoulder, "I'll be back soon!"

I was now alone for the first time since I ascended, and sighed looking at my beautiful gown.I needed to shower before I changed and it would help me think, clear my mind of Gideon and the strange overwhelming connection that I felt with him. So, with a shower in mind, I went and checked my bathroom out—it was a drastic improvement from the tiny dingy stand up shower I had in my apartment on Earth—and like everything else in my house, it was what I had envisioned. Perfect. Complete with a stand up shower, jacuzzi garden tub, white granite countertops and sand colored tile floors. There were fluffy white towels and an array of oils and soaps to wash with. I twirled around, "Oh, it's PERFECT!"

After my shower, I felt a million times better clean, relaxed and rejuvenated. I stood in front of my closet and grabbed the gown holding it up to my body. This was the first time I had looked in a mirror since before I died. My reflection shocked me; I was more beautiful as an Angel than I ever was as a human. My plain brown eyes were much larger now—Jade green with swirls of Amber—gorgeous and motion filled like Gideon's.

I pulled my eyelid down examining them, it was strange, but I liked it. My hair was long and filled with lustrous waves. It cascaded down my shoulders and arms. Before, it was always flat and uncooperative—I had hated it. I looked like a new and improved version—I was still me—just not the *human* me, I was an Angel. The thought made me smile.

I slipped the gown on and stared into the mirror satisfied. It was no surprise how it fit; molding to every curve of my body. I stood there playing with my hair trying to match the elegance of the gown but gave up after a few failed attempts at an updo, I settled with a quick French braid to pull it back out of the way. Nodding with pleased approval. “Hm… not bad, not bad at all.” I said as I checked myself out. I had never been vain but then again I had never *felt* beautiful like this—or more comfortable—in my own skin.

I walked to the windows in my bedroom, opening them up so I could look out onto the ocean. Taking it all in one last time before heading out—a part of me still warring with the notion that I would wake up—that this was all nothing more than a very vivid dream. I stared out the window—the sun's rays reflected off of the water creating little prisms of rainbows and energy—and prayed that this was real.

“Nice view.” I whirled around, Gideon was leaning up against the door frame of my bedroom. His arms folded in front of his broad chest. He was wearing the same thing he had on when he left—apart from the robe—he looked heartbreakingly perfect. I nodded dumbly trying to find my voice. “I love it—but didn't you have to go get changed? You're wearing the same clothes.” He smirked, holding a finger up. “No, I said I had to ‘get *ready’*—and I did. Follow me Love—I have a surprise for you.”

We walked over, I had to fight the huge smile that wanted to cover my face. He had gotten a surprise for me, maybe he liked me too. How would I ever know? What was I going to ask? ‘Oh hey, are Angels allowed to date because I know we just met and all but I think you're my soulmate?’ Ridiculous. There I was, acting like a schoolgirl fantasizing about my crush, throwing around terms like ‘soulmate’ I couldn't seem to help myself. Gideon was special to me, and he made me *feel* something I had never felt with anyone else in a way I couldn't ignore.

I wasn't sure how much longer he would be with me but I knew it wouldn't be the 'forever' that I desired. He would have to leave the moment Jesus felt I had adjusted to Heaven and would no longer be in need of his guidance. There would be other Angels ascending by then— they would need him just like I do now—those were the facts, the facts were easy.

The hard part came from what I didn't know: How I would cope with saying goodbye when the day came, how often I could see Gideon after he left, where our friendship would stand, and all the unknowns that would stem from there. The thought made me anxious, but I pushed it out of my heart and let it go, it did me no good to worry.

For now, Gideon and I got to spend almost every second together, and I refused to let tomorrow's problems ruin today. "Are you ready guest of honor?" He bowed and extended his hand. "Oh, why yes, sir." I Curtsied and accepted it laughing at our foolishness. "M'lady," he rolled his hand—continuing our role play—and cleared his throat. "Your chariot awaits." He opened the door and led me onto the porch.

"Oh my—" I looked at Gideon in disbelief. In front of my house there were two gold horses with a small open chariot attached to them. He wasn't kidding about the chariot. "I thought everyone flies in heaven? How did you—get horses—and a chariot?" I asked. Gideon was smiling as big as I was and looked pleased with himself.

"I thought you might enjoy this... we're taking— the scenic route. You'll appreciate it, I'm sure." He looked at me shrugging his shoulders. "But we can fly if you would rather—" I put up my hands to stop him from talking "No! Are you kidding? I would *love* the scenic route!"

I love flying, but no way am I turning down a chariot ride with a gorgeous man-Angel at my side. Nope. The chariot was all white with gold trim I ran my hands along it, admiring the details. There were bouquets of lilies on both sides tied up and fashioned with silk and ribbon. *Magnificent.* The horses fascinated me the most.

"These horses are beautiful" I was in awe, they looked like they dipped them in gold. Their mane and tails were shimmering like liquid silk. "Yes, they are. We can ride anytime you want, just to clarify— flying is the *preferred* mode of transport, not the *only* one, Love." He gave the side smile that I loved and with a small crack of the reigns and we were off.

It may have just been wishful thinking, but I got the vibe I wasn't the only one who had stronger than normal feelings—I was sure that Gideon had them too—maybe not *as* strong as mine, but he had them, I could feel it.

CHAPTER SEVEN: PARADISE VALLEY

The road was brightly lit and shimmered as if they had composed the dirt of glitter. We rode for a while and Gideon pointed to random landmarks in Heaven. Mountains filled with colors, homes of other Angels, fountains, parks and of course, the brilliant watercolor sky with the brilliant diamonds above us. I grabbed Gideon's arm in a panic as I looked ahead and realized the road ended. "Watch out!" I warned, fearing we would fall off the side of the planet.

As we got closer, I noticed there was actually a wall of transparent white light with rainbow sparked streaks moving a million times per second through it. "What happened to the road—what's that shiny stuff?" Gideon grinned as we picked up speed, heading straight toward the wall. "You'll see!" I covered my mouth to keep the scream in and braced for a collision closing my eyes.

I held them shut for a few seconds—opening them when I felt a shimmer around my body—we had gone *through* the wall smooth as a hot knife cutting butter. *What just happened?* "What is this place?!" It was unbelievable. Unimaginable.

Everywhere I looked, there were hundreds of thousands of huge transparent spheres. They shined like bubbles but were reminiscent of snow globes because each bubble contained houses and people. There were children running and playing with each other and picnic tables filled with goodies. Some bubbles had houses both big and small. Some set in hot sunlight, others covered in snow or showing the ever beautiful colors of fall—no two were alike. There were so many of them—I couldn't count them all—I looked at Gideon awaiting an explanation. "How is this all real? What is this place?"

"Well—all Angels have a greater purpose of service here in Heaven—so we have to communicate, train, and interact with one another. But, as I told you before Love, not everyone who dies becomes an Angel. When an average person—when someone who was not chosen to be an Angel—passes away, they have a similar walk-through and welcome you first received. They see the glory, the wonder, and create their own home. The *only* difference is, once they set their reality, they're saved here in their sphere where they can spend eternity in peaceful bliss. We call this place Paradise Valley, everyone is separate in their spheres so their realities don't interfere with one another's."

He leaned in, "The last thing someone who desires summer year round wants is to have a blizzard at their door because so-and-so up the road loves the snow!" We both laughed.

It was hard to wrap my head around—the 'regular people' got to stay in their own little 'happy sphere' forever—what about Angels? And as an Angel.... what would my forever entail? I stared at each home and saw their happiness, bubbled away safe and sound and felt a twinge of envy thinking about my uncertain future in Heaven.

Why did I have to be an Angel? Paradise Valley would be a much simpler way to spend eternity. We continued our ride to dinner—passing by hundreds more spheres—and I watched the scenes of happiness play out feeling a little guilty for spying on people's lives.

"So why do we see everyone? I mean, once they're here wouldn't it make sense for us to never see them again?" I asked, wondering if Gideon was getting sick of answering my never-ending questions yet. He didn't seem to mind but a part of me thought it might bother him a little to always have to answer *something*.

"Well, we can see them because we're Angels." He pointed to all the spheres floating in the surrounding atmosphere. "They may go for eternity without ever needing us. But who knows, one day intervention might be necessary. Darkness has a way of sneaking in. Even in the daylight, shadows remain. We have to protect all aspects of Heaven and remain vigilant for their safety, and ours. No worries though! Angels train to deal with any threats to protect Heaven at all times."

How could there ever be a threat here? It's Heaven, it's supposed to be peaceful for eternity, isn't that the point of Heaven? *"What* could be a threat?" again with the questions, but I just couldn't help myself—I *needed* answers. "I mean, isn't Heaven supposed to be all 'peace and serenity forever and ever'?" Before he could even respond, we came to another white wall which I presumed would lead us out of Paradise Valley. I turned around in my seat taking one last peek so I could see all the happy bubbles people created.

"Yes, well, it's *supposed* to be and, it has been" He paused looking at me. *What changed...* "Don't worry Love, you're about to get your answers because, we're here." We continued through the wall to our destination. *Just when you think you've seen it all...*

CHAPTER EIGHT: THE HALL OF WARRIORS

A grand white building floated in the center of a magnificent garden flowering bushes and trees surrounded it.The dome-shaped roof of the building was covered in Gold with millions of diamonds that reflected the sun's rays, sending streaks of vibrant color in all directions. I noticed six pillars of marble were in every corner, on each was a statue of an Angel kneeling with a sword. Maybe they were in mourning or paying respects.

Fountains fed into glass paths, filling them with sparkling blue water, and met up to form a circle beneath the building where I saw colorful fish swimming throughout. "Whoa." I walked underneath, straining my neck as I tilted my head up to examine the bottom of the building. "Cool..." Gideon followed me under, "You know, you are the strangest girl I've ever met. We arrive at the place that will give you your answers and rather than go inside, you go exploring.." He ran his fingers through his hair smiling at me, tousling it before dropping his hand. He was too beautiful for words—the soft light emphasised his chiseled features—showing off his strong jawline, perfect skin and his eyes, under this light they were radiant.

I narrowed my eyes at him playing off my infatuated gaze and continued my investigation. "No, I'm the most curious… so does this stuff make it float?" Galaxy slime—that was what it looked like to me anyway— blanketed the bottom of the building in a shimmering liquid. The soft light came down onto us giving our skin a light blue glow. "Yes, it is what makes it float, a little creation of God's to reward us with a beautiful place to meet." He answered, taking a step closer. I froze as his hand touched mine and the familiar shock went through me, my body humming, yearning for him.

“It's much more interesting inside, shall we?” he pulled my gently by the hand, escorting me back to the open garden. “We gather here to make our plans and preparations.” He released his wings and I followed suite, it felt good to stretch my wings, like the first stretch of the morning after a hard night's sleep.

“Are you ready?” I nodded, I was ready to see more, to learn more, and knew the answers to my questions lay just beyond those doors. More than anything I longed to understand my purpose here. *I'm ready.* I took a deep breath, and we made our ascent to the Hall's entrance. The two large doors of the entrance were made of solid gold and carved with the scene of a battle between Angels and Demons. There were gruesome images of both Angels being slain by Demons and falling, and Demons being slew by Angels and cast down. A tremor of fear—perhaps intuition—shot down my spine like ice.

At the center of the battle scene I thought I recognized one warrior on a horse wielding a large sword encased in flames and pointed to him. “Is that Jesus?” He looked so fierce and strong—hardly recognizable in battle gear—but it had to have been him. “It is—you're very observant.” He smiled, confirming my assumption his face exuding pride for our leader. Jesus was remarkable for more reasons than one could count, “He has been the leader of God's army of Angels and sole defender of Heaven since he ascended. Our Father tasks him with the responsibility to lead, train and recruit us. Every one of us Angels has been hand-picked and selected for the various gifts that God has given us to create the strongest defense possible and eradicate all threats we may face—” He looked at me.

“He will be able to tell you more though—” he gave me an excited smile. “Are you ready to discover and embrace the purpose of your existence?” With the question came a sudden wave of stage fright. I stared at him, a blank expression on my face. I couldn't answer—or speak yet. There's been a mistake. What could I offer Jesus' army? What was expected of me? I sighed, standing at the door wouldn't lead to my answers. “Well—I'm as ready as I'll ever be.” I muttered as we pushed through the doors.

There were hundreds of Angels inside, some of them I recognized from the training field but most were faces I had never seen before. All the female Angels were wearing the same gown I was, I looked down at myself smoothing my dress. *At least I made the right wardrobe choice.*

The Hall was just as enormous on the inside as it appeared to be on the outside, Angels made their way to the long tables that wrapped around every side of it. The floors were a polished marble, white and shined. There was a huge statue of Jesus centered in the Hall with the six Angels—the same ones I had seen on the pillars outside—they were holding their swords up high as if heading into battle. *My God...* I wondered if they recruited me to fight. That would *definitely* be a mistake— I had fought nothing in my life—it was not my forte.

"Jacey!" I heard a familiar husky voice call out and turned to find him. "Jesus!" I smiled, still in awe—being able to say his name and see him in front of me—it was the most unreal experience of Heaven by far. It even trumped Paradise Valley and the ability to create things with your mind—and that was a big one. He wrapped me in a warm embrace then pushed my shoulders back to look at my face, he grabbed my hands. "Come, sit with me, I would like you to meet someone." and led us to the corner of the table where another female Angel sat.

She stood up to hug me with a bright, enchanting smile. "Jacey! I'm Zahara. I cannot tell you how excited I was to find out you had ascended!" She was beautiful, no, gorgeous—like an Amazon princess—with long silky dark hair and bronze skin. Her eyes were like mine—a bright Jade green with swirls of amber—she would put Aphrodite to shame with her looks.

"Hello, it's so nice to meet you Zahara." I reached to shake her hand—she bypassed it and wrapped me in her arms—then pulled me to sit down beside her as if we were old friends. Jesus motioned to the enormous spread of food that lay before us on the table. "Before we begin, would you like something to eat? Or drink perhaps?" I shook my head and put my hand up, all I wanted was to ask my questions and find clarity. "No, thank you." Without being hungry I really saw no reason to eat—that would just delay my quest for answers—and I felt I had waited long enough already.

Gideon tapped the table with his fingers like they were drums and licked his lips. "Well, *I* do!" He piled his plate, and I laughed at his eagerness. "Wow, you *can eat*!" I said, somewhat shocked to see someone who wasn't hungry devour so much food. Jesus burst in hysterics. "I told you!" He slapped Gideons stomach shaking his finger at him, "You're lucky—" Gideon rolled his eyes "I know—I'm lucky I can't gain weight!" I joined Jesus laughing as the object of my affection warded off the jokes of our leader.

He swallowed hard and then spoke. "I don't care, poke fun all you want! You're the ones missing out! This food still *tastes so good*. And besides isn't that what every woman dreams of on Earth? To be able to eat whatever you want and not gain weight?" He eyed me with a disarming wink that embarrassed me and took another bite. "Don't mind me—" He finished chewing, "Talk, I'm not going anywhere, Love." I grinned every time I heard him call me 'Love'.

I looked over to Zahara and Jesus—they seemed to be whispering to each other—preparing to bombard them with my questions when Jesus turned to me and spoke. "Gideon has told you that you are a Healing Angel correct?" I nodded. "Yes—but I still don't know *what* that means—or how I belong in any part of *all of this."* I motioned my hands to the Hall all around us.

"Well, your role Jacey, as a Healing Angel like Zahara here, is to fight for Heaven's safety and protect everyone in it with your unique gift. You can heal the Angels afflicted with the venom of evil and any other injury. You and Zahara are the only two of your kind, sadly, we have lost all the others."

Jesus appeared lost in thought for a moment then looked into my eyes. "Do you want to hear a story?" unable to speak, I nodded. Heal Angels from the venom of evil? Who ever heard of evil having venom?

CHAPTER NINE: THE STORY OF LUCIFER

Jesus took a long drink from his cup and began his story. "Angels are unique now because God used to create them in their original form right here— in Heaven. They knew no life on Earth, only what they saw in glimpses of humanity and it made them lack compassion and understanding for man. God began creating 'children of light' as we call them after he had cast Lucifer down— after his betrayal.

"God wanted Angels to have a deep love and compassion for mankind just as he does. He figured the best way to ensure that would be to make his Angels walk the Earth as humans *first.* When they ascended—or die as you would put it, they would get their wings and fulfill their destiny according to their various gifts.

"The problem is that Lucifer's demons have been targeting and corrupting the Children of Light for centuries now, those destined to be Healing Angels are at a much higher risk because a Healing Angel is the only cure for the venom of evil. They are priceless to this Army, to me. When the venom infects an Angel and they are not cured, it is a fate worse than death. You burn first, then your life-force leaves your body but you remain— empty, a shell of nothingness—you become one of Lucifer's Fallen, driven and filled by evil.

"Ironically, Father created the first of the Fallen— he thought he was being merciful—his act of mercy led us to where we are now: on the precipice of war." I placed my hands to my face, covering my mouth as I let his words sink in. *This is unbelievable. Not only am I recruited into God's army as a Healing Angel, I'm also on the top of Lucifer's hit list and incapable of fighting. Wow. That's not terrifying at all…* Jesus looked at me and sighed.

"You see, Jacey, what humans know about Heaven is that this is where you go after you die, after you have been deemed worthy to spend eternity here ever after." I nodded, "Well, what humans *don't know* is the cost of that eternity of happiness and peace… Angels get to experience their own form of Heaven, a less 'ignorant' state of Heaven, so to speak.

"We know of everything that goes on, and have to remain vigilant, there is a constant threat—and it came from God's most merciful act—he has lingered, plotted, and corrupted. We must face, and conquer this threat, it is our duty to set things right and protect Heaven at *all costs.*" I was shocked and terrified. Lucifer. Of course he would be the threat everyone has been referring to, and they wanted to *fight him?*

But I didn't ask for this duty! "What do you mean all costs?" None of this seemed fair, they recruited me and *expected me* to just give up my eternity of happiness to fight in some war? I was all about serving God but to die again? I didn't know if I could handle that.

"There is always a cost, every choice or action no matter how small or big— has consequences." He looked at me and raised his eyebrows. "You're familiar with the story of Lucifer right?" I thought back to my earlier years in Sunday school. *God's most beautiful Angel; he was jealous of God and tried to turn everyone against him. God cast him down to spend eternity in darkness thus creating Hell. yada yada yada...*

I looked at Jesus "Yes....?" It came out as a question. I was sure that what I knew and what Jesus knew were two very different things. "Well, there is *much more* to it than you could ever imagine." I was right. "So listen and you will understand *everything.*" I adjusted myself in my seat and took a drink of my cup fidgeting was a nervous tick I had carried with me from childhood but I tried my best to sit still. "Okay," I sighed, sitting on my hands. "I'm all ears."

"Lucifer was the most beautiful Angel God had ever created, well-loved among the Angels and favored by God. However, all the love and praise given to Lucifer from God was not enough to make him happy because he was jealous of God's love for man. He didn't understand why the need to build an inferior form of beings if not for servitude. He wanted the power, the worship, the love— he wanted *everything God had.*

"He had become obsessed, demanding God give him more knowledge and learned all he could about the power we share we call it our life-force. Angels share life-force with God and he shares his power with us. Lucifer learned how to control his own life-force for evil and used it to manipulate others. He experimented and Angels came up missing after Lucifer discovered how to steal their life-force to absorb it, making him grow more powerful-"

I was lost in his story, playing it out in my mind as he spoke, I could almost see it.

"God loved Lucifer so much, that he couldn't see the darkness growing within him— even when the trusted Guardians told him of the incidents with the missing Angels and their suspicions about Lucifer." *This is new.*

"Lucifer was trying to gain as many numbers as he could to serve under his rule, so he planted seeds of jealousy against God among his group of Angels. He taught them how to control and absorb life-force but with more followers stealing life-force, more Angels went missing. It was a mystery. No one knew where they had gone because with their life-force stolen, it prevented their ascension into Guardians therefore cutting off all communication to God.

"They became *powerful* and planned on rushing God's temple and stealing his life-force from within him and promised his followers they would share God's life-force, enjoying ultimate power and everything that came along with it," He paused before continuing as if the story hurt him to speak it.

"They came one night, and God saw the true evil that had consumed them as they battled. They were much more powerful than God had thought possible and they fought on throughout the night. God and his Guardians against Lucifer and his followers. There were many Angels that lost their lives battling to protect God with everything they had. God and what the last of his Guardians detained them and to make an example out of them, God took back his life force, leaving them nothing but emptiness.

"The traitors felt pain, sorrow, hunger and thirst and without God, they would never again know relief from their afflictions. The beautiful Angels that God had created were now gone, instead they were monsters showing on the outside the dark ugliness they had within them and they became the first of the Fallen; the first demons."

"But with Lucifer, God's heart hurt the most, he couldn't bring himself to destroy his most beautiful creation. So instead he stole most of his life-force and cast him down to rule the desolate underworld you all know as 'Hell'. Lucifer's blatant hatred of mankind would be his ultimate punishment; God would banish him to live and walk below the humans he thought so little of."

Jesus looked at me and placed his hand over mine, "God's great act of mercy by not destroying Lucifer has now brought life to Heavens greatest threat." He shook his head, "Lucifer learned that *any soul* gave off some of God's life-force and with it, more power; so the more souls condemned to Hell, the more power he gained. The fewer souls that ascend into heaven, the less power God has.

Our situation and our Father's has grown dire, he's grown weak from lack of life-force, and with that weakness comes an opportunity for Lucifer; and he knows it."

An electric tingle shot down my spine—I didn't want to fight Lucifer—the mere thought of it turned my stomach and the more I knew, the deeper that fear sank in.

"As the years have worn on, Lucifer has become stronger than you can ever imagine. With more lost souls, Fallen and countless demons he is stronger than the first time he tried to steal God's life-force. And God is weaker now because so many Children of Light are turning to darkness before they can ascend into Heaven.

"His plan from the beginning was to rule from Heaven's throne, stealing away mankind's free-will, making all of humanity bow down before him as slaves; or suffer the consequences." He paused and took another long drink before continuing. The table had gone quiet and the Angels near us had diverted all of their attention to Jesus as he spoke. I figured they had heard this story a thousand times before—but judging from the way I felt—this was a story you wanted to hear *every* time someone told it.

CHAPTER TEN: THE PROPHECY

The Hall fell into complete silence as Jesus spoke again, "Man has always been my father's first love. His perfect creation, even when Adam and Eve disobeyed him and introduced the knowledge of sin to humanity, my father still loved them. As did I, I went down to earth to save all of man and I was successful in opening the gateway to Heaven to them once more."

He looked at me, I nodded showing that I was still following. "When I was born, Lucifer did everything in his power to stop my ascension and when that failed, he came up with a plan. He would have a child conceived and birthed from pure evil. A son that would lead an army of demons strong enough to rise against God and his Angels and overthrow Heaven.

"There is a prophecy of this war between myself and Lucifer's son, his name is 'Damien' It is said that we engage in the most gruesome battle any world and any realm has ever known. I fear with mankind almost consumed in sin, Lucifer is as strong as ever and we are at the precipice of that prophecy coming true." I was shocked and fearful as I realized the severity of the situation.

War could come? I then thought back to the golden doors at the Hall's entrance. "Didn't you already battle before? What about those carvings on the doors, and the statues?" I asked.

Zahara, who had also been sitting engrossed in Jesus' story, answered for him. "The battle is foreseen by the Watcher Angels—they posses the gift of sight. The images are of what is yet to come, not of what has passed." She reached over and grabbed my hand and a soft gold and green glow shone between us. "You see this light?" she asked, and I responded with a nod.

"Well, this light is your gift. It helps you heal and create. We will teach you everything you need to know and prepare you for the battle. We need you Jacey. It is up to us to make sure that Heaven stays safe. We must fight for those who cannot fight for themselves--- We have the gift of Healing, they gifted us with this ability to save the lives of our fellow Angels on the battlefield who otherwise would have perished."

She was speaking of our role with pride and I envied her confidence. "We are talking about fighting Lucifer himself and his army of demons! I don't know if I can do that!"

Gideon reached over and held my hand; I calmed down and took a deep breath. "Don't worry Jacey, we will help you, you'll be ready for anything by the time we get done training you! Trust me!" But I didn't want to die, I wanted to spend eternity in peace.

"I've fought nothing in my life! You do not understand what you're saying— what you're asking! I'm trying to tell you, it's wrong, you have got the wrong girl— I don't want to fight!"

Gideon looked at me, concerned. "I know you're scared, love----we all are. But you need to understand Angels only have to worry about the venom of evil, you're a Healing Angel remember? So that's taken care of for you! When an Angel perishes by any other force they ascend again, they lose their physical form and ascend into Guardians. They stay with God as pure energy and regain their physical form only when he sends them down to earth to watch over and protect their charges.

"The charges are Children of Light; people who will ascend into Angels one day. So, it's like a circle of life." He drew a circle in the air with his finger and rested his hand on mine, "You need not be afraid, they train us, and will train you for anything. Do not fear ascending, it's an honor, and just know that you will still be you no matter what level of existence you are at." I felt like I understood, at least mostly.

Gideon continued, "The Guardians sole task is to ward off the demons and preserve their charges right to ascend. Guardians differ from Angels in the sense they are much more powerful. They have a strong link with God's life-force and can ward off the demons after the Children of Light."

"What happens when they can't defeat the demons after their charge? Did I have a 'Guardian'? You're not a Guardian though... right? So how does that work?" Gideon looked away for a second, a flash of pain shown in his eyes. My questions hit a nerve with him, a twinge of guilt hit me in my stomach.

I was being difficult and selfish for no reason. He shifted in his seat, "Nobody knows what happens to them. We call them The Lost Guardians We never see or hear from them again. Yes, you had one, but he disappeared along with many others. We're down to the last six Guardians and they must stay with God. Some Angels, myself included, have stepped up to protect the charges." I didn't know what to say, 'I'm sorry' didn't seem good enough especially when he had done nothing but help me, so I sat in quiet thought.

CHAPTER ELEVEN: INVASION OF PRIVACY

I looked at him for a minute. So I am Gideon's charge... That must be why I feel so connected to him. I mused feeling slightly relieved that I wasn't abruptly turning into some sort of stalker. His face showed pain, I wanted to comfort him in the same way he had comforted me through all of this. I touched his hand softly and tilted my head to meet his eyes—they were filled with loss—I smiled tentatively.

"It's going to be okay," I said working hard to keep my voice level and reassuring, "Whatever comes our way—we'll face it together—and then we'll find a way to save the Lost Guardians and bring them home too." I was pleased with how confident I sounded. I didn't have the slightest clue of how—or if it was even possible—but I smiled encouragingly until he smiled back.

I felt sorry for questioning Gideon, it seemed I dug up a painful memory by asking about the Guardians. *Maybe he knew one who had been lost?* It was time to start asking the right questions—ones that would lead to me accepting and understanding my destiny—as a Healing Angel, I would be trained to fight in God's Army and I had to learn to live with it.

Around the Hall all of the Angels were standing tall and exuding confidence. I turned my attention to Zahara, she was the key to my understanding this whole Healing Angel business. "So...how long have you been a—Healing Angel?" She thought for a moment, "Well, ever since my ascension." I liked how she said 'ascension' instead of 'ever since I died.' Ascension just *sounded better, less morbid.*

"I'm not sure how many earth years I have been here. But I do know that all of my memories as a human seem fuzzy and distant now." She continued. I could see how that would happen and thought about my human life—I hadn't mourned my old life or family since I arrived—and wasn't sure if that was even possible, to mourn when I felt no real sadness. I remembered my mom, she had raised me with help from my grandmother until she passed. I was an only child, no siblings to miss and had made no friends in school. Reminiscing kind of filled me with wonder; how did I let my human life pass me by without ever making any real connections? And how did I make such an intense and immediate connection with Gideon and Jesus—even Zahara—who I barely met?

I guess because as a human I was always so focused and driven to become a doctor that I barely lived my life when I was there. I did miss my mom though as I thought about her sweet face and gentle way. She was funny and erratic but worked all the time to support me and my dreams—she was probably heartbroken over my death—I shuddered and pushed the image of her crying at my funeral out of my mind. That would do me absolutely no good. I guess I could have cried... maybe screamed if I thought of it too long. I could have run or flew as far as my legs or wings could take me but it wouldn't make any difference—I had died— there would be no turning back.

My human life was just a grain of sand on the beach of eternity and this—being a Healing Angel in God's army—was my forever. *I have to be okay with this, I don't have a choice*. I felt bad—I wanted to embrace being this coveted healer but fear was not my best friend—and everything was happening so fast, it was crushing me. The more I found out, the more I wanted to run for the hills. Each time I felt confident, something else came up to knock me back down. I wondered if I was really ready for any of this. Maybe I was just kidding myself by believing that we had a chance, or that I could actually help in any way.

Gideon, reached over placing his large hand on mine, as if he knew I needed reassurance. "It's a lot to take in Love, but *you* are going to do great things here! You were *made for this!*" Although acting was never my strong suite, I thought I was doing a pretty good job holding myself together, but Gideon saw right through my façade. He knew what I needed, and always said the right thing.

He was my gravity right now and I was so absurdly thankful to have him. I chose my words carefully—attempting to sound nonchalant—and kept a smile on my face, "I know, I'm just trying to get the feel of things, here." *And drive someone else crazy with my nonstop questions.*

"You don't drive me crazy Love." I snapped my head to face him. "Huh?" I didn't say that out loud. There's no way I said that out loud. Did I? I recalled my thoughts and my words—I had most definitely kept my thoughts in my head—I remember choosing my words carefully for a reason. "No, you didn't say anything out loud. I can hear everything you think." He said it as if it was no big deal—just a regular conversation—but he had a smirk on his face that was impossible to hide. He knew everything I was thinking. He was *smug.* I stared at him with my mouth gaped open fumbling around for some semblance of a coherent thought and got nothing.

"What the—?" My voice was barely audible as I choked on the words I took a breath. "*How*—wait so, you—*can*—*you*—*hear my thoughts?"* I didn't even understand the convoluted sentence I had formed—so I was surprised when he answered—and still shocked. "Don't be alarmed. I *am* your stand in Guardian ...remember? You're my charge hearing your thoughts makes it easier to discern how you're adjusting. It helps me know what you *need* in order to help you. It's a good thing!"

I hit the table with both hands pushing myself back in my chair. "That is a complete and total invasion of my privacy!" I stood up furious and thought about leaving but changed my mind when I realized I didn't even know my way *anywhere.* I sat back down begrudgingly dropping my face into my hands.

"How could you *not tell me that you could hear my thoughts?!"* My words were muffled as I was too embarrassed to lift my face. Yet again, I was thankful to be dead already so my face couldn't flush. I probably would have looked like a green eyed tomato right now. I kept my face hidden, feeling utterly mortified.

"Ah...Don't be embarrassed, love" Gideon comforted. "It's only temporary." I lifted my face, feeling relieved. "Really?"

"No, not really. I'm sorry. I was only kidding." Everyone burst out laughing—obviously having fun at my expense—and I threw my head back down to hide in my chagrin. "Ugh!" I growled.

"We can *all* hear each other's thoughts." Zahara said through laughter. Jesus cleared his throat placing his hand on my back rubbing it gently his voice low and soothing. "Jacey —it's all right— Angels are all connected this way. When you ascend, you take and give life force in Heaven. This unity gives us our great strength." He put his fist up in a triumphant motion.

"In all seriousness though," He continued, "this link was a 'fail safe' that God created in all of his new Angels after Lucifer betrayed him. With shared thoughts, no Angel could ever be corrupted and go unnoticed again." I understood the concept but one major point bothered me. "Well, if we can *all* hear each other, then why can't *I* hear any of *your thoughts?*"

Gideon gave me an apologetic look. "Well, you haven't tried yet Love." I couldn't believe my ears. *I haven't tried yet because I didn't know!* "That's because *you didn't tell me to!"* I practically shrieked. *Ugh! this is pointless. Oh, wow why didn't I think of that myself?* I sulked silently.

Why didn't I just focus, 'ooooh I want to read Gideon, and Jesus, and Zahara's minds what on earth are they thinking' I was making the facial and hand expressions to go with my thoughts, as if I was speaking the words aloud, which apparently I technically was. I imagine I looked much like a pissed off mime. The childish ranting in my head made everyone around me laugh hysterically.

I eventually recovered from the embarrassment and laughed too, I couldn't help but to be overwhelmed with the giggles like the rest of them were. I guess it *was funny.* Besides, now I knew I could also hear thoughts—someday when I tried or was taught—and that seemed pretty damn cool to me.I decided to keep playing the mind reading game. '*Oh that's alright just wait'* I thought loudly so that everyone could hear me. *'Wait until I can get inside all of your heads! And I'm not asking permission either! Eavesdropping time!'*My threat brought about yet another round of laughter.

We laughed until we couldn't speak or breathe. I looked at all of their faces and felt such love in my heart.You can't pick your family on earth or when you're an Angel, but I couldn't have picked a better one for myself. Gideon's charm, Zahara's kindness, and Jesus' strength—I loved them all so deeply—and I would do anything for them.

CHAPTER TWELVE: GIFTED

Jesus stood up, "Are you ready to meet the rest of your family?" I popped up next to him—winded from laughing—and ready to stretch my legs. "Lead the way!" He held his cup up, tapping it to get everyone's attention before he spoke. "Angels, Please assemble in your separate groups." The Angels complied standing in front of the tables along the Hall.

We walked over to the far end where a group of large male Angels gathered, "These are the Warrior Angels, Gideon is their leader. Their specialty is close quarters combat. If you want to know how to maneuver or fight your way out of a corner, these are the guys to show you how to do it." I waved, they were all large and strong reminiscent of gladiators or Spartans and shared Gideon's mesmerizing blue eyes. Our eyes have something to do with whatever gift we have—that's why mine are Jade and Amber—like Zaharas. We continued moving on to the next group.

"These are our Messenger Angels. They are the fastest out of all of us; they can get a message across the battlefield in the blink of an eye— just wait until you see these guys in action." Jesus nudged me with his elbow. He exuded love and pride as he talked about each of their gifts like a father would speak of his children. The Messenger Angels were smaller and younger built for speed, not battle I presumed.

A blonde-haired boy stepped forward in front of me, “Hi, I'm Colin!” He had fair skin and light freckles across his face. “Hi, I'm Jacey” I shook his hand looking at his eyes, curious about my theory. Sure enough, they differed from mine, and Gideon's, Colin's eyes were a deep chocolate brown with gold lightning streaks flowing around his pupil. “I'm the leader of the Messengers,” he put his hand up to hide one side of his mouth and whispered, “*and the fastest* so if you need anything, let me know!” I laughed “I will.”

Jesus tousled Colin's hair. “All right Colin, back in line.” The young boy stepped back getting shoved around by his comrades, ‘you're the fastest huh?’ and ‘Yeah right I could take you in a race any day’ the other boys he stood with said. I loved watching them play with each other; the sight of their liveliness warmed my heart. I wondered how it would feel to belong to an entire group like everyone else had or if my group would remain with just Zahara and I.

The next Angels were female with a few males scattered within them, their eyes looked like liquid silver or platinum. “These are our Arsenal Angels— our weapons specialists so to speak. Arsenals create some of the most fantastic and powerful weapons one could ever think of, imagination is their gift, and it is incredible! If you need any weapon, or know one, they are the Angels to see to create *anything.*”

A tall and thin girl stepped forward smiling, she had short black hair like a pixie and ivory skin. “Such a pleasure Jacey, I'm Eliza, the leader of this broad!” she motioned to the Angels standing behind her, I nodded. “Ask for anything! I'm sure we'll see a lot of you in training, but if you need anything, please don't be shy or nervous!” She hugged me and stepped back into her group. *Eliza.. a weapons specialist. Colin, a Messenger, and Gideon and the Warrior Angels.* I needed a notepad and paper for the amount of people I needed to remember, not to mention each of their various gifts.

After a quick ‘Hello’ to everyone, we moved on to the Watcher Angels who possessed the gift of sight. They were the strangest so far with eyes almost twice the size of mine, like a galaxy swirled around their pupils. Watchers could see *everything*, far enough to catch glimpses of things yet to come; they were the Angels who foresaw the battle between Damien and Jesus and my ascension, which is why Gideon said they were ‘waiting for me’.

We approached the center of the group. “Jacey, I'd like you to meet Maleki” Jesus introduced an Angel standing in the front as he stepped forward, “Hello, nice to meet you.” I shook his hand. He was a large man, with dark brown skin and deadlocked hair. He held my hand for longer than the traditional handshake staring at me for a minute. *Okay…* He released my hand with a brilliant smile. “You will love it here Jacey! It's nice to meet you in person.” He had a thick accent I couldn't quite place.

Maleki had a familiar sense to him; I felt as if I already knew him even though we had just met. I waved goodbye, locking eyes with him again before we moved on. The eerie feeling he knew me a little too was hard to shake. *Stop being paranoid, everyone will think you're weird.*

We came upon the final group of Angels and they were *huge*— even bigger than the Warrior Angels, with amethyst eyes swirled with white. *Oh. My. God.* I was staring, but I couldn't help it, they were beautiful, and mysterious looking. Something made me want to bask in their glory and learn everything I could about them. Jesus stood in front of them showcasing the group with his hands, "These are our Elemental Angels." A tall woman stepped forward extending her hand, she had vibrant red hair pulled back in a French twist. She had a sophistication to her, an ancient knowledge held in her eyes.

"Hi Jacey, it's good to meet you! I'm Ashira, the leader of the Elementals." I shook her hand, stammering, "Hi-um—hello Ashira, I--" I shook my head. *Get it together.* and took a small breath "It's--- it's good to meet you." I got out.

Why am I so nervous? Geez. They were all so big and gifted, it was rather intimidating. Ashira smiled, "Oh, don't be nervous dear! We're no different from you!" *Except for way bigger, and more gifted and stronger.* "Um… what does an Elemental Angel *do?*" Jesus didn't introduce them like he did the others. *I wonder why…* "Well," Ashira turned, motioning for another Angel to join us. "Corey here will to show you a little something of what we do."

She nodded to Corey, he had dark black hair and creamy skin, he looked like he may still be in the young teens. He stepped up beside her taking a wide stance and braced his feet while making a swirling motion with his hands, a small funnel of wind took form in front of him like a tiny tornado. The funnel grew larger, the winds it emitted blew around us with a vengeance my braid whipped around throwing pieces of hair in my face and I squinted my eyes shut. With a clap of his hands, it was over, I opened one eye Corey beamed at me as I applauded him. "That's incredible! Great job!"

Ashira touched his shoulder, dismissing him back into the ranks with an approving nod. "Thank you Corey." She said and turned back meeting my bewildered gaze. "We Elementals control all four of the elements; Earth, Wind, Fire, and Water." All I could do was shake my head and stare with a childlike wonder. Ashira laughed, amused at my expression, "There is *much* more where that came from! That's nothing, dear! Tomorrow during training, you will get to see everyone at their best!" It filled me with a new sense of confidence and I was eager to train to see what my *powers* could offer the group and what I could learn from the others.

Although the prophecy still terrified me, I was embracing my destiny wanting to learn as much as possible, so we could be ready for whatever Lucifer had planned. Seeing all the Angels and what we could do made me feel certain that together, we could handle *anything.*

CHAPTER THIRTEEN: PATIENCE

We made our way back through the crowd and the Angels mingled again talking about various exercises and different techniques to apply at tomorrow's training session. I sat down at my seat thinking to myself watching Jesus speak to others around us.

Angels don't keep track of time; they have no clocks or calendars, and never get tired, or hungry. So how we know when to start and stop training? Lost in my mind again, I was oblivious to the fact that my thoughts may not be private.

"We begin at daylight and stop when we feel like we have gotten more skilled." Jesus said as if answering someone's thoughts was just common practice. Before I could scold him he continued, "Sometimes we train well into the night, I have had this *feeling* like we are running out of time like we are on the cusp of disaster. Maleki and the other watchers see nothing, it worries me.." Exhaustion showed on his face and I felt bad for the overwhelming weight Jesus must be carrying.

He looked at me, the stress of his thoughts weighted heavy in his eyes. “Perhaps Lucifer has gained the power to move beyond our watchers sight.” He shook his head

“Oh,” was all I could say.

He smiled, "I’m sorry—I know you still have to get used to sharing your thoughts and didn’t mean to make you feel uncomfortable, we’ve all been sharing thoughts for centuries so it's hard to remember that you have yet to gain that skill or become comfortable with it." His words were sincere. "It's not a big deal, no need to apologize." I said.

“You will be much happier when you can master communication, I can show you now and you can exercise it more with Gideon on your own so by the time training ends tomorrow you’ll have gotten it down pat.” It was music to my ears, I jumped up. “Yes! That would be fantastic!”

Jesus faced me in his chair. “Okay, the first thing to know is that we can only listen to Angels close to us, second, it’s easier with someone you are familiar with because you listen for their voice.... *their inner voice.* Third, it takes an immense amount of concentration, the process gets easier the longer you are here so don’t worry if you cannot get the hang of it right away—*you will.*” I nodded.

“Focus on what my voice sounds like, listen for it.” It felt strange staring at Jesus and trying to get inside of his head but I focused all of my energy until my ears rang. “Nothing.” I said.

"Shh—Close your eyes and *focus. Listen to my voice..."* His voice drifted off into a whisper lower, and lower, I clung to it in my mind.

'*Hello----- Jesus?'* I focused and heard more nothing. *This is ridiculous.* "Im sorry but I hear nothing*!*" It was frustrating, and my mood was clear on my face.

Jesus patted my shoulder. "No one gets it the first time... Being connected takes immense concentration and a strong bond." He paused for a moment. "You'll get it like nothing soon I'm sure, we can try again during training tomorrow—speaking of which, we had better call it a night and get you back to your house so you can relax because tomorrow, the *real fun* begins!"

He was right, how could I expect to master everything when I had just found out I was a recruit in God's Army this morning. Patience eluded me, just like in my human life when I jumped into college, then grad school without even a break in between because just so I could rush to the finish, start a new life. Everything was a rush, impatience was a part of my personality, something to work on as an Angel; patience is necessary if you will live for eternity.

Jesus stood up and clapped his hands. "Angels, my brother and sisters! Let us say goodbye for the night. Go home, get rest and I will see you all on the training field tomorrow! Thank you all for welcoming our new sister into the family with such open arms. I love you all. What a fantastic celebration, Goodnight!" The Angels all clapped yelling 'we love you Jesus! Welcome Jacey!'

they whooped at the top of their lungs and moved around heading towards the doors to exit the Hall.

CHAPTER FOURTEEN: LEFT IN THE DARK

Gideon, who was mingling with the rest of his Warrior Angels, said his goodbyes and came back over to where Jesus and I were. He was doing a light jog, smiling as he made his way to us. He had a brilliant smile and his big ocean like eyes made my knees weak how someone I met could have me gushing over him was an utter mystery yet here I was admiring him at every turn.

I remembered that my thoughts have never been private since I ascended and embarrassment filled me; I had been swooning over Gideon since the moment I saw him and he had to have known. Mortified at that realization, I averted eye contact and focused on not thinking anything as he approached us, Jesus spoke first so I took the opportunity to recover.

“Gideon, please take Jacey home and make your rounds through Paradise Valley when you're done, you can take Colin with you to get it done faster, tomorrow is a big day for all of us. Our Army is complete with Jacey here.” He wrapped his arm around my shoulder and squeezed.

"Oh! I want to see Paradise Valley again! Can't I go too?" I couldn't wait to see the magical land of happy spheres and wondered what 'rounds' entailed. Jesus' face went from calm and happy, then angry. "What do you mean again?" Jesus looked at me and glared at Gideon who avoided eye contact. "You took her to Paradise Valley already?!" He snapped. "You fool! Do you realize what you may have done? What this could cost us? What were you thinking?!"

It confused me and I was desperate to help Gideon. "It's okay. I loved it. It didn't freak me out or anything, it was great!" I mean, there were nothing but thousands of happy bubbles floating everywhere so why was it such a big deal, why couldn't I go there? Jesus glared at Gideon again and seeing him angry was scary, I knew why he was such a good leader now; no one wanted to deal with Jesus when he was upset.

"I'm sorry sir." Gideon said his face full of chagrin. "I—I thought she'd be fine, I knew she would like it, and it was on the way---" Jesus scoffed, holding up his hand cutting Gideon off mid-sentence. "That was NOT *your* decision to make!" He snapped. I stepped between them. "What is the big deal?" I would do anything to spare Gideon from Jesus' anger.

Gideon spoke. "If an Angel sees Paradise Valley before they have accepted their role in God's army, it can sometimes hinder the assimilation process—we've lost Angels before to the draw of Paradise Valley. That is why we hide it—and we keep it hidden until you've—adjusted. It helps the process along, makes it easier to accept your destiny if you don't see—what you're missing out on."

I gasped, I had heard everything Gideon had said but only *one thing* stood out and I had to ask. "What do you mean you've 'lost Angels to Paradise Valley before'?" Jesus answered, "You have a choice. Free will and all... you may have been hand picked and created for this purpose, but the choice to accept it or not---is still up to you." Excitement rushed through me with the revelation. *I have a choice!*

"Yes." Gideon looked up at me. "Every Angel passes on, or accepts---all of this." He motioned around the Hall and continued. "But there is a standard we must follow before we reveal Paradise Valley to any new Angel. We give you a tour, have a dinner to celebrate your arrival and then we train you for a week, after they form the bond we give the choice." Gideon looked as if he were searching for something in my eyes; he was unsure of which I would choose.

"We want every new Angel to see the value and gift of what we do *first*. Yes, it is a sacrifice, but one that's *worth it* for the greater good, it is an honor to be an Angel, but it's tempting to choose Paradise Valley." Now I understood why Jesus was angry with Gideon; he thought I would choose Paradise Valley because I didn't have time to form a bond with the Angels. The truth is I didn't know what to do, and there were many factors to consider before I made my choice. Until now, I thought I *had no choice, and* this was the hand they dealt me, and I would have to spend eternity fighting Lucifer and his demons.

That didn't sound very appealing compared to the blissful state of Paradise Valley, but I already loved my new family and couldn't imagine spending eternity away from Gideon. Paradise Valley would be perfect if I could have him there with me but he made his choice now I had to make mine.

I stood in the middle of them still and silent; careful with my thoughts as I did not want to take the chance of stirring things up again. "Excuse us for a moment Jacey." Jesus pulled Gideon to the far corner by the gold front doors, they spoke to one another glancing in my direction. *Great.*

I didn't know what they were saying, but I knew it was about me. At first it appeared Gideon disagreed with something that Jesus had said, shaking his head and running his fingers through his hair and appeared agitated. Zahara, Ashira, and Maleki came over and joined in on their discussion. Gideon looked unhappy but nodded, conceding to whatever the group was saying.

I wish I could read thoughts already. I stood watching, feeling insecure about my being excluded. They looked up from each other and I looked away ashamed they caught me staring. Everyone walked my way, whatever they had discussed had made them all happy, Gideon and Jesus were smiling and relaxed again.

"Change of plans Jacey" Jesus said. "Tonight, we will take you somewhere special." Zahara came over and placed her arm around me, giving me a gentle squeeze. "I'm so excited for you Jacey!" enthusiasm in her voice. I smiled. Everyone was smiling and excited, but I still felt confused and left in the dark.

"Where—where are we going?" I asked. "We'll talk on the way." Gideon answered. "No worries Love, It's a long journey, there'll be plenty of time to explain."

'*Good.*' I thought trying to project my words into his head, unsure if it would work but it seemed logical that if we could go into each other's minds to listen, we could send our thoughts straight to them, '*because I have a lot of questions.*' Gideon smiled. "You always do," I felt a rush of excitement. *It worked!* I rather liked that I could talk to him even if the others could hear me.

"Are we ready then?" Jesus asked everyone as he turned towards the doors. "Let's do it!" I hoped to sound as optimistic as possible. We stood out on the patio in between all the marble pillars. We were hundreds of feet in the air and had a perfect 360 degree view of the land all around us. The sky was gorgeous as usual, covered in vivid pink and gold with streaks of orange, teal and violet streaked the trees with shining leaves of brilliant colors.

The sun was setting, it left a soft light and created a golden hue on everything it touched. "This way, let's go guys." Jesus ordered as he leapt into the sky and his wings emerged. One-by-one we jumped, following Jesus to my unknown but 'special' destination. I pushed myself up to where Gideon and Jesus flew together, leading the group.

With the promise they'd explain where I was going while we were on our way, I wanted answers and I would not wait any longer. "Where are we going and what's going on?" I asked, cutting to the point. They exchanged a look that made me wonder what they were saying in their heads to each other. "Just tell me." My patience was non-existent and their cryptic secrets made me uneasy.

"We are taking you to the Well of Knowledge--" Jesus stated matter-of-factly, as if that should satisfy me for an answer. "What's the 'Well of Knowledge' and where is it?" I pressed for more information. *I think I deserve an explanation.* "It's in a desolate part of Heaven; the original Garden of Eden, God abandoned it after Lucifer betrayed him and Adam and Eve ate the forbidden fruit. It is a dead garden now but there is one priceless thing that exists among the remains: The Well of Knowledge." He looked at me smiling as if that answered everything.

I couldn't help but to smile back even though it still confused me, Jesus always put me at ease, it was his gift. Now I wondered why this 'Well of Knowledge' was significant, or how that would help me and why did we have to go tonight?

"You know, I'm thinking I'm asking all the wrong questions." I said with a hint of sarcasm. "Oh? Why's that Love?" Gideon asked. I put my hands up shaking them; exaggerating my frustration. "Because *none* of my questions give me *anything* but *more questions.* I get no answers and never have a clue about what's going on around here!" Everyone laughed at my outburst.

"Well, I don't think it will be an issue after this." Gideon said. "You'll have *all* your answers." I hoped he was right, there was a lot to think about in the days ahead and a huge choice to make. Paradise Valley alone in bliss or A Healing Angel in love with an unattainable soulmate serving in God's Army, fighting for my existence.

CHAPTER FIFTEEN: THE GARDEN OF EDEN

We were flying for a long time enjoying the beauty of Heaven when the sky grew darker and I saw a patch of dead land coming into view. *Oh, my God. This can't be a part of Heaven.* It stuck out like a sore thumb. There was nothing but black and gray rocky turf, dried-up riverbeds, and barren trees. It looked scary and eerie; A chill ran up my neck and I got goosebumps just looking at it.

I pointed to it, "Is *that* where we are going?" The whole place looked wrong; everything about it screamed that it didn't belong here in Heaven. Jesus nodded, "Yup." as we made our descent into the abandoned garden. Maleki, Ashira, and Zahara landed walking around the area checking around the large rocks and into the caves and crevices. The carefree and fun loving Angels I had just met now looked like they were ready for a fight.

"Um—is everything okay? I mean, are you guys—looking for something?" They were scouring the surrounding land. "They're securing the area to keep us safe." Gideon said. "Safe from *what?*" Their paranoid behavior frightened me but Gideon placed his hand on my back and rubbed between my shoulders, it calmed me. "From anyone or anything that shouldn't be here. Don't worry, it's what we're trained for." A chill shot down my spine and I looked around in fear, the darkness surrounding this place was enough to make my skin crawl.

Jesus came into view from a high ridge above us "Are we clear to move forward?" Maleki and Zahara nodded to Ashira who answered, "Clear down here." He motioned for us to follow him and we all flew up to the ridge. "The Well is down there." he pointed to a large cave tucked between two mountainous walls of rocks. In its glory, I imagined there was a raging waterfall, with rainbows forming as the sunlight caught the molecules in the mist, it was there to hide God's chambers. But like everything else in The Garden, it dried up and died... lost to time and forgotten about ages ago.

There was more evidence of dead beauty all throughout the abandoned Garden of Eden. Trees that were once lush with color, were now grey and black. There was no grass through the valley either, just dead soil and a dried up old riverbed. My heart was heavy with a sadness as I looked around at the depressive state God left the garden in. To think once upon a time a valley so filled with life and love could now be so devoid of it; it showed God's sadness.

Maybe that was why he left it that way; as a reminder of what his creations were capable of. The evil that exists within mankind and Angel kind alike, despite his selfless love for us was a lesson he would not want to forget. *This sadness and his pain was clear all around Eden.* I understood God a little better being in that place, it reminded me of our mission and my never-ending quest to understand what was going on. We walked through the valley and stopped at the entrance to the old falls.

Jesus turned to face us. “Ashira, stand watch out here with Zahara and Maleki. Gideon and I will take Jacey to the Well.” He looked at me. “Are you ready to have your answers?” I swallowed the lump in my throat and gave a tiny nod. Gideon took my hand and squeezed it, extending his other hand to show me the way. “After you.” And we all walked into the cave.

It was pitch black inside. The darkness where you can see nothing. I put my hand out in front of me to prevent from walking into a wall and took cautious steps as not to trip. I bumped into Jesus when he bent down with his hands on the ground in front of me. “Oh! I'm so sorry.” I heard him laugh, “No worries, just a second...” He grunted, and I watched in amazement as dozens of orbs lit up along both sides of the path, lighting the way for us. Each was free floating and put off a shimmering blue white light.

I wanted to touch them but refrained, they were bright and beautiful and I thought I would break them. Jesus walked down the narrow path as we followed close behind. Gideon was still holding onto my hand and I was glad he was there with me. It was always better with him near me. We walked in silence until we could go no further. There was nothing but a wall of rocks. *Okay… what now?* It appeared as if this part of the cave had collapsed.

"How are we going to get through there?" I asked Gideon. "I wouldn't worry about that—watch this." He pointed to Jesus standing in front of the wall, he threw his arm down and a large silver sword engulfed with white flames materialized in it. He thrusted it into the wall and gave it a twist like turning a key and the wall peeled back, vanishing before my eyes. My mouth dropped in shocked amazement.

"Whoa! You have got to teach me how you did that!" I pointed to the new entrance. He raised his eyebrows, his arms in front of him and motioned for me to step through the entrance he had created. "After this, I might not have to." Before us laid a grand room untouched by time... God's original chambers.

I walked around staring at every inch, looking at every detail, it was the most up close and personal experience I had with God since my ascension. The brightness of the chamber seemed so out of place compared to the rest of Eden; every surface of the room looked like mother-of-pearl, bright white with an array of other beautiful colors shining through. It was astonishing.

Jesus stood in the center of the room in front of a gold decoration on the floor that looked was reminiscent of the NorthStar. "Come, time is not on our side in this circumstance." There was an urgency in his voice I had not heard before and I wondered if it had something to do with whatever the others were searching for earlier. He took his sword and traced the outline of the star, leaving a white glow where it touched and lifted it up high to drive it down into the stars center and stood back.

CHAPTER SIXTEEN: THE WELL

Beams of bright white light shot out from the floor followed by a rumbling that shook my entire body. Terrified that the chamber was collapsing, I wrapped my arms around Gideon, his face shown the same confusion I felt. "What's happening?" I asked trying not to sound as frantic as I felt. "I don't know--" Gideon looked around checking for signs of collapse and held me close to him. "We're— I think we're moving... up."

The walls got smaller and smaller, I closed my eyes taking deep, calming breaths. When the rumbling ceased, I opened my eyes to find it had lifted us into the sky. There was no ceiling, no walls, and no windows just four pillars with large globes on top of them glowing. I saw a white chaise lounge between two of the pillars and in the center of the floor where the star had lain in the previous room, now lay a glistening pool of water with hundreds of galaxies swirling within it as if the water was a living milky way.

It was, much like everything else here, unlike anything I had ever seen before. *It's beautiful...* I stepped forward and bent down reaching out to the water. "I wouldn't do that if I were you." Jesus cautioned. I pulled my hand back and looked up at him.

"So what do we do now?" I asked. Jesus walked to the chaise lounge and patted the space next to him, I followed and we sat together. "The Well of Knowledge is powerful Jacey, it takes only a drop and once you drink from it, it will change you forever. You will amass far more knowledge than you could come to know, and this knowledge is *significant* to you— so that you may understand our dire situation— and the magnitude of whatever your choice may be." Gideon and him exchanged a look. That must have been what they had discussed earlier, he must not have wanted me to drink from The Well—but Jesus did and I trusted he knew what he was doing.

"It was upsetting to find out about your seeing Paradise Valley before, because I could sense that envy had already touched your heart. The truth of the matter is, we *cannot* afford to lose you Jacey, although you have a choice to decline being an Angel, it is still your destiny. The draw of peace and happiness in Paradise Valley is strong, I understand that, but the fate of our Father, all of Heaven and Earth, is at stake."

It filled me with chagrin to hear his words because they were true, I *felt* envy for the deal that others had gotten and wanted my own happily ever after, not a war and eternal servitude. But that didn't mean I *couldn't* embrace being an Angel, I believed in my heart I would rather be conscious and aware of my surroundings than in a euphoric state of ignorance for all eternity, anyway.

"It's not *envy per se*," I began. Jesus raised his hand, stopping me before I could continue. "There's no need to explain yourself Jacey, *we understand*. We have all been there and had similar instances and experiences." He laughed lightly, "Do you not think we too, wouldn't prefer an eternity of peace? To no longer live in fear of what may happen?" He leaned in close and held my hands between his.

"But you see Jacey," he continued. "That makes what we do so important, what your choice and every new Angels choice *means to all of us.* The magnitude of this war is beyond your comprehension and that's why you are here; to gain the wisdom necessary to understand *everything.* It can be intense— but I am sure you can handle it. You know that the war we are about to fight is not for nothing, it is not just for our sake, but for everyone's sake *we must* defeat Damien and Lucifer. This is bigger than you—than all of us and the only chance we have at a victory is to face these demons—together and we need you."

Gideon walked over to the well and knelt down beside it. A small silver chalice raised from the center of the water and he grabbed it and brought it over to us. "We will be here every step of the way for you Jacey." He said.

Jesus stood up, "You should lie down." He directed. I laid back terrified. "What will happen?" Gideon leaned over me placing both hands above my shoulders, his face inches from my own. I felt a rush of excitement from his closeness and forgot about my fear. "Think of it as an out-of-body- experience, you'll see things like you are watching a movie, but it will connect you *to everything.*"

Jesus sat on the edge of the lounge swirling the fluid in the chalice. "It only takes a sip, so just relax and allow it to take you away." He held my head up, allowing me take a drink. The liquid filled my mouth, it was cool and thick, I closed my eyes and swallowed. The darkness behind my eyelids grew deeper and billions of beams of colors shot around in it.

I could feel the water moving throughout my body traveling everywhere inside of me rushing through my veins. My body went numb, and it took me away, I felt no presence of time or physical being. More darkness formed like a tunnel, it drew me in. I then saw myself, laying down with Gideon and Jesus by my side, it looked like I was sleeping.

Gideon was right, this is a total out-of-body experience. I looked down at my hands, to my amazement, they were transparent and glowing with radiant rays of amber and white energy. *Whoa.* A sudden rush of wind came around me spinning fast, an immense pressure surrounded my astral body and it sucked me into a portal. *What's happening?! Where am I going?*

Terrified, I grasped at the air trying to stay in that room for fear of what may lay ahead. *"Help! Please somebody! Jesus! Gideon! Help!"* I screamed as It sucked me deeper in. *"It's Okay, love. Just let yourself go…"* I heard Gideon inside of my head. A bright flash of light came, and I left.

CHAPTER SEVENTEEN: ENLIGHTENMENT

The light surrounded me; I had to shield my eyes away from it unable to stop myself as there was no solid ground to stand on. I continued free floating through the portal with no control. Stay calm. Stay calm. I'm okay. The pressure decreased, and the brightness dimmed down. I exited the portal and watched as everything around me formed.

At first, it was a distant blur, but as the brightness receded, my eyes adjusted and my surroundings came into focus in sharp detail. How strange... I was back in the Garden of Eden to my great surprise however; it was not the desolate and dead place we had just walked through. No, this Garden of Eden was vibrant, and exuding life. I was in a time warp and focusing was difficult as everything was coming and disappearing in rapid flashes before my eyes.

I watched and my mind absorbed everything I saw. Another bright and blinding flash of light swirled around me, I found myself in God's chambers standing only three feet away from him; God himself, in his human form. Oh, my— I wanted to touch him and reached my hand out towards him as he dashed by me.

No, I'd better not. I pulled my hand back as he passed me and looked at him, taking in every detail of his face.
He was an older man yet appeared to be in peak physical condition, had vivid turquoise eyes like Jesus with a small amount of white facial hair and wore a long white robe. He paced around his chambers, troubled by something with two tall male Angels talking beside him.

Their words echoed and were unclear; as if they were speaking, and I was under water. But in my mind, there was no confusion. I knew what was being said even if I couldn't hear it. The Angels were warning God of Lucifer's plot to destroy him and takeover and told of his followers.

The group was growing, and they all had suspicions about Lucifer's involvement with the mystery of the lost Angels. They wanted God to leave until Lucifer was detained and fervently made their pleas to him putting their arms around his shoulders to escort him from his chambers. God demanded they leave him as he shook them off angrily and they warned him again of Lucifer's plan, accusing God of being blinded by his love and favor of him.

Distressed upon hearing this, he threw his hand up to stop the Angels from speaking anymore. He told them they were just rumors and ordered them to leave with a dismissing wave of his hand. Everything moved in a blur, followed by another flash of blinding light and again, the scene came into focus.

I watched in utter horror as Lucifer and his followers rushed God's chambers. Lucifer was every bit as beautiful as one could imagine. He had alabaster hair, shoulder length, slicked back and held at the base of his neck in a ponytail. His skin was a creamy beige, free from even the slightest imperfection.

He was the largest Angel I had ever seen, bigger than Jesus and the other Angels with a strong jawline, prominent chin, chiseled features and ivory white teeth. His eyes glowed a fierce silver with hints of blue and violet. I had seen no one or anything like him. God and Lucifer now stood face-to-face

. God's face showed no anger, just hurt, and love, the sting of this betrayal clear in his sad turquoise eyes.
Yet Lucifer stood proud with his envy and hatred of God all over his face.

How could he hate someone who loved him so much? He was speaking to God, disgusted by his creation of inferior humans. They were the superior beings; if God was to make humans, Lucifer believed they should make humans for servitude, nothing more. The free will of the humans would cause absolute chaos as they could not trust us to communicate and make choices.

God explained that we were to be his children just as the Angels were and we were to be loved just as he protected and loved them. This angered Lucifer even more and he attacked God. Oh no! I clasped both hands to the sides of my mouth in complete shock. This can't be happening...

He ordered his followers to grab God's arms, and they obliged. They stood there holding God leaving his chest open and vulnerable. Their faces showed no emotion and were blank of expression; they looked like robots. Lucifer placed his hands on both sides of God's face and his eyes went black as coal as he pulled God's own life-force from his body. Bright beams of white and prismatic rainbows began to drain from Gods chest where his heart would have been circling and forming into a ball.

No! his life-force!

I knew how this ended, that Lucifer would be cast down and God would overcome but seeing it happen before my eyes, it made no difference what I knew before. From where I stood, God was losing, and it wasn't fair. There were too many of them, God could not fight them off himself. Where are all the Angels?

I went to the door to see if anyone was coming to help God. The sight I came upon was that from a horror movie. I clasped my hand over my mouth to keep from screaming. Dozens of Angels lay slain throughout the path leading to God's chamber. Their eyes wide open but empty and black. Their faces twisted from the agony of their final moments alive.

I could see black streaks all throughout their bodies and faces. As if someone filled their veins with ink. Is this what they suppose us to face? This was not the ascension they promised to an Angel who gave his life. This was agonizing pain, and sheer terror. Where are the other Angels? Where are the Guardians?

I turned around going back into the chamber. God was near death, I could see his face drained of life. There was nothing I could do but scream, “No! Stop it!!!” This was too much, it was heartbreaking. I couldn't be quiet, I was sobbing with a broken heart for God's betrayal.

Lucifer hesitated as if he had heard my cries and for a split second, his eyes met mine. He locked me into this piercing stare and I froze as time stood still. Can he see me? Everyone was frozen—except Lucifer. His lips curled up into a twisted smile again and my heart sank into my stomach— he can see me.

It was only a moment and then everyone moved again. I questioned the plausibility of what I had just experienced. Maybe my eyes were playing a trick on me. There's no way he can see me! God couldn't even see me! Gideon said it would be like watching a movie. That means I am just witnessing what happened.

This isn't happening in real time…
Just as it almost finished him, draining God's life-force, Angels rushed to God's aid, turning the tides of this battle in his favor. The Guardians. They were enormous and transparent like I was and wielded large swords like Jesus' and moved with lightning fast speed. Yes! Yes! Get them! I cheered. Another flash of light came ending the scene.
I saw God standing in front of Lucifer and his followers.

The Guardians held them on their knees before him. I watched as God stripped them of their beautiful wings burning them away, absorbing their life-force, and leaving the exiled Angels mutilated and powerless. He opened a hole in the floor and cast them down without mercy.

God held Lucifer longer, he caressed his cheek followed by a sharp back-hand across the face. He placed his hand on Lucifer's large chest and it looked as if he were pulling his life-force from him. Yet, God stopped and Lucifer laughed at him. I couldn't look away though I wanted to. Lucifer was taunting God for his weakness, in my heart I was cheering God for his strength.

God held Lucifer's chin up to look him in the eye as he explained to him what lay ahead for him: An eternity of darkness: where he would never walk in Heaven or get to live higher than the so-called inferior humans; now, he would be lower than them. Destined to watch from below as humans walked and lived above in God's favor.

This, God hoped would teach him humility. For no being is greater than God, they are all equals, they are all his children, and they are all loved. God kissed Lucifer's cheek and Lucifer spit in his face his one final act of defiance and disrespect. God stripped his wings away and cast him down through the fiery portal in the chambers floor. It's the same spot where the Well is now.

Another whirlwind like flash came, and I was standing at a large tree in front of a beautiful dark haired and very naked woman. This must be Eve. I watched her step forward smiling as she admired the fruit of the tree. I stood there as scenes played out around me.

Eve and Adam biting the apple, the serpent in the tree, God's disappointment in the humans lack of self control, the creation of life on earth, Jesus being born and ascending.

I understood every moment, memorized every detail and felt all of it as flashes came and went: humanity's problem with sin, the Guardians fighting off the demonic influences of Lucifer, Angels ascending into Guardians, humans ascending into Angels, I was witness to it all.

In another flash, I saw the war; Damien and Lucifer's army. I saw the sheer size of it and it made a sick feeling stir in the pit of my stomach. I watched the fire and war go on between Angels and Demons in fast forward motion.

I saw Angels laying slain on the battlefield in blurs and Zahara and I rushing to aid as many as we could. The ones we couldn't get to ascended but demons were trapping their life-force in these strange cylinders taking our fallen comrades away with them.

The battle scene was intense and graphic; I couldn't take seeing any more of it. I covered my eyes sobbing and screaming, "Enough! No more! I don't want to see anymore!" I heard Gideon's familiar voice in the distance. "It's okay Jacey. You can come back now. Jacey----- wake up!" I opened my eyes to see Jesus and Gideon's faces and sat up hugging them, still weeping.

CHAPTER EIGHTEEN: THE POWER OF KNOWLEDGE

I pulled myself up to a sitting position, trying to collect my thoughts. I trembled, beads of sweat collected on my forehead and my breath was shaky. "Do you want to talk about it?" Gideon asked, I shook my head. "What did you see?" Jesus pressed, I sat for a moment thinking about what I had to do.

The battle was coming and the fate of the universe depended on *us* winning, how could I hide like a coward in Paradise Valley? Besides, even if I chose Paradise Valley, when the war came—and it *was* coming, if we weren't victorious, they would lose Paradise Valley—forever.

There's no other way. "I made my choice— to be a Healing Angel, to protect Paradise Valley, and all of Heaven and Humanity." I looked at them for a moment before it came rushing out of me like a damn that broke, "The battle is horrible! I saw it! The Angels—they—we lose so many and they don't ascend! The demons, have these—these *tubes,"* I held my hands out showing the size and shape of the cylinders with my hands "they—they trap the Angels life-force so they can't ascend!" My breathing was ragged, I tried to control my cries so I could speak.

"That's where all the Lost Guardians are— they take them! I don't know what they do with them it was awful! There were so many of them, so many of *us—falling!* Zahara and I, we couldn't save everybody!" I shook my head, "Couldn't get there in time! We weren't fast enough! I don't know when—but I *feel it*. And we're not ready yet! *I'm not ready yet!"* I was sobbing harder— my words falling out of me as I looked up with tear-filled eyes, "Do you understand what I am saying? We need to do something! We're not ready for this!" I cried.

There's not enough time. What are we going to do? What am I going to do? "Calm down, it's okay." Gideon wrapped his arms around me and rubbed my back as the tears kept rolling out. Jesus sat for a moment, reading my thoughts I guessed, but I was too distraught to care. I now understood the magnitude of this situation, I understood the reality of all too well.

We aren't all going to make it. And even worse, there will be no ascension for those of us that don't, no, Lucifer has made sure of that with--- whatever those tubes were. What will happen to all the Angels trapped? I didn't even want to know.

"Take deep breaths Jacey, collect yourself—we need to go." Jesus ordered, I looked up, he was not the comforting Jesus I had gotten to know, he was determined and stern. It was time to be strong, I wiped my eyes, blew out a deep breath and stood up, "Yes, sir." We had to train and fight, and I needed to be a *soldier* so we could stop Lucifer from succeeding in his plan. We *would* protect Heaven and Earth, or die together trying.

Jesus walked back to the Well and placed the chalice back in its center the floor sank back down into the lower level of God's chambers. We left the room and Jesus covered it again, concealing it behind a wall of rocks. Being back on the path I remembered the dozens of Angels I had saw laying lain on the floor the night Lucifer had made his betrayal and shuddered.

We exited the cave and met up with Zahara and the others, Jesus walked up to them and turned to face Gideon and I. "Gideon, take Jacey home, stay with her as long as she needs, there's something I must do," He looked at me, "Rest tonight, don't worry, I *promise you* we will be ready and you will too." They flew off disappearing into the night sky.

Gideon looked at me, concern washed on his face. "Are you ready to go home? We can stay for a while longer if you feel you need to rest more…" I took a deep breath and looked up at the sky. There were three moons in Heaven, all different from the one on Earth. They speckled them with an array of colors glowing throughout and like the sun, one was much larger while the others were smaller and seemed distant. The sky would bring me peace while flying, and I needed some of that right now.

"I'm ready," I rubbed my arms and shook my head, "I can't stay here any longer, I want to go home." Gideon nodded, "Okay, let's go." And we left the abandoned Garden of Eden, forever, I hoped.

CHAPTER NINETEEN: FEAR OF THE UNKNOWN

Neither of us spoke as we made our way through the clouds but it was a comfortable silence, just his presence was enough for me to feel the anxiety lift away. The more miles I put between Eden and myself, the better I felt. As we approached my house, a wave of utter exhaustion hit me, it was in my head, but it still seemed real.

I wanted rest but rest wouldn't be in my future, there was too much to think about and I needed to figure out what I had saw, what it meant, when the attack would come, and so much more. Even after drinking from the Well of Knowledge, the only thing I was certain of, was there would be a war and Lucifer was the epitome of evil and I already knew that beforehand. The missing detail of *when* that war would be, would drive me crazy until I felt we were ready, that *I* was ready and who knows how long that would be? Right now, I couldn't even handle getting home by myself let alone fighting a demon.

"I can stay with you for a while--- if you don't want to be alone." Gideon offered as we walked up the steps of my porch. I smiled, he knew what I needed, and I needed help to process everything. I remembered his rounds through Paradise Valley. "What about Paradise Valley? Don't you have to go make rounds?"

"Don't worry, I will," he said "*after* I make sure you're okay." It relieved me, I wanted him to stay at least for a little while. We walked up the stairs and I turned to look at him, "Thank you, Gideon — again, for everything—it means a lot." and invited him in. We walked inside and the tension left my body I was finally at ease; my home was serene and peaceful. I went and got a box of tea out, it may not have been a necessity, but it was a habit from my previous life that comforted me. *This is just what I need.*

I looked at Gideon who was already sitting on my couch, reading the book he had picked out earlier. "Tea?" I offered, shaking the box. He looked up from his book and smiled, "Do you have any honey, love?" I materialized teddy bear honey in my hand, a favorite of mine. "Sure do!" I held it up showing off my creation. "You know, you're getting good at that." He gave a nod of approval.

"Why thank you--" I turned to the stove, put the kettle on, and got two mugs out. "--I learned from the best you know." I walked over to my French doors and opened them up, letting the salty air move through my house as I stepped out onto my deck. *This feels good.* There was a light, cool breeze that came and went in perfect harmony with the waves as they crashed against the shore.

God, it's so peaceful out here I pray we can get through this... whatever is to come, please give me strength to fight. What happens when Lucifer's wrath falls upon us? How can I stop something when I don't even know when it will come? Do I live an eternity in constant paranoia? Please, keep me strong God. Help me get through this.

I leaned on my banister looking out onto the dark water focusing on the gentle sound, and watching as the moon appeared, and disappeared behind the clouds that rolled by in complete silence. Alone with my thoughts trying to let the calm of the ocean wash over me, I had all but forgotten the tea and jumped at the screaming sound of the kettle whistling. *Oh!*

I hurried through the doors and into the kitchen, Gideon was already in there turning off the stove. He turned around with both cups in his hands and looked up at me. "I'm sorry love, I didn't know if you liked honey or not so I put nothing in yours." He said. "It's okay, I take nothing in my tea. My grandmother used to tell me that 'It's best if you don't mess up a good thing; you can't appreciate something if you change it.'" Gideon blew into his cup and took a sip, looking up from it at me. "Smart woman."

I grinned, but the smile faded as my ears rang followed by a searing pain through my head. Something triggered in my head and hit me with flashes of Lucifer and the war from the Well — I became dizzy, my body numb, and the cup of tea slipped from my trembling fingers, shattering on the floor.

The ringing grew so intense I felt that my head would explode, I placed my hands over my ears but the hurt intensified. *It's coming from inside of my head.* "Oh my God!" I screamed in agony. "Jacey! Are you all right?" Gideon rushed toward me concerned, the ground shook beneath my feet and the walls of my home crumbled in a bright red fire before my eyes.

I reached for Gideon but he vanished along with the rest of my home and surroundings. The ringing faded, and the pain subsided leaving me groggy and disoriented.

What's happening? Where am I?

I opened my mouth to yell for Gideon but no sound would come out like I was on mute. My throat burned as I tried to scream louder and louder for help.

Gideon! Gideon where are you? Help me! Somebody please help!

Fire surrounded me, and Gideon was nowhere I looked all around but saw nothing but glowing embers, I could feel the heat burning my skin and opened my wings to make my escape. A soft male voice surround me. "I wouldn't do that if I were you--" I scanned every corner and crevice of the smoldering room but saw no one.

Who's there? What do you want? Where's Gideon? Where am I? I demanded. The voice was right behind me now, whispering in my ear. "I'll answer whatever questions you might have my sweet, sweet, Jacey but first--- we should have a proper introduction." I jumped as two hands came over my shoulders grabbing me, whirling me around. *Oh no!* It was Lucifer.

I was standing face-to-face with *Lucifer.* His eyes glowed an eerie black with shimmers of silver and red. He was no longer the beautiful Angel who walked by God in Heaven, no, *this Lucifer* looked pure evil and his demonic appearance terrified me.

He smiled at me and caressed my cheek, I cringed at his touch but did not dare move; He froze me with fear. "Ah, that's not very polite you know." He tsked at me, feigning offense, dropping his hands.

I have to get away. There has to be a way out. As I turned to run away from him he was in front of me again smiling, I jumped back with my hands shielding my face in fear. *Stay away from me!* "You're not going *anywhere*.... yet."

He laughed and moved closer again. Lucifer had trapped me somehow and I could not escape. *How did this happen? I'm an Angel. You can't keep me here! Where's Gideon?* I had never felt more alone in my life, and he just stood there watching me, laughing and smiling; my torment, entertained him.

Jesus! Jesus! I screamed inside my head.

Lucifer's face grew angry, he wrapped his hands around my throat lifting me up, my feet dangled in the air, I thrashed trying to fight back but it was futile. His hand went around my chin and he squeezed, holding my face still and leaned in closely.

"Jesus... *can't help you, Jacey"* He snarled, curling his lip with disgust.

His breath felt hot against my cheek and opened his mouth as if he would bite me and I struggled. My eyes widened as his teeth grazed my neck. *Oh no!* He brought his mouth to my ear, snapping his teeth shut with a loud clap.

He was toying with me, feeding on my fear. "You are *mine.*--Do you understand? We have a—history, you and I." His face grew soft, and he set me down, I dropped to my knees, clasping my throat and gasping for air.

I looked up at him, angry now. *No! I am NOT! You are EVIL!! You can do whatever you want, torture me, kill me, I will NEVER be yours!*

Lucifer looked indignant and scoffed. "I will not do any of those things Jacey! I wanted to offer you something… a deal if you would." He rolled his hand towards me. "Your precious 'God and Jesus' offer you servitude and certain death, if you face me. You saw only a glimpse of what I can do-" His lips pursed as he caressed my face again, I turned my face away.

"I don't want that for you." He shook his head looking down at me as if he pitied me. "I want to offer you an *opportunity*…. This one time. I will give you *a new life with your precious---"* He looked at me, narrowing his eyes as if in thought, "*Gideon was it?"* My heart dropped into my stomach. *Oh my God does he have Gideon?* He smiled.

"No war, no strings all you have to do…. is *leave—together.* You will get to be with your prince charming and have your little happily ever after and no one will bother you again." He walked around me, circling as he spoke.

"It will be just the two of you, *safe* and *free*..." leaned in whispering, "It won't take much to convince Gideon to run away with you. He has the power to leave Heaven, you know." I shook my head fighting back the offer though it truly tempted a small part of me.

No... I won't betray them. We will fight to stop you! Lucifer smiled. “Think about it----” He rushed towards me in a blur holding both sides of my head, bringing his mouth to my ear he hissed, “See you soon, Jacey.” I felt the floor disappear beneath my feet and everything went black as I fell into the unknown, screaming in terror yet trapped in silence

CHAPTER TWENTY: DEAL WITH THE DEVIL

"Jacey... Jacey wake up!" Gideons voice echoed around me and opened my eyes to darkness and placed my hand in front of me to feel for a wall or something. *Gideon?* I tried moving my arms all around but felt nothing— no ground beneath my feet nothing above, or around me.

The darkness felt creepy and made my hairs stand up on my body as I felt a dark presence with me. *Where am I? Hello? Gideon? Can you hear me?* "What's the matter with her?" It sounded as if he were yelling from the top of a canyon; by the time his voice reached me, it was barely intelligible. "Do something!" He sounded frantic.

Wake up? He said I need to wake up. So, I must be asleep I need to wake up! Rubbing my eyes hoping to come out of this dream hurt because I was already awake. Lucifer must have stuck me in the abyss; a place of dark nothingness with no way out. I heard ragged breathing and a low growl. *Oh God!* There was *something* else in the abyss and I could *feel it watching me.* I sobbed as worst-case scenarios rushed my mind.

Who's there? I looked around, but the darkness had swallowed me and without my sight it felt like my entire body had vanished. The only part left of me, was my consciousness. *There's nothing here. It's just your imagination.* I tried to calm myself down ignoring my goosebumps and rationalizing the strange sounds. *It's all in your head.*

"Jacey," It was Jesus I heard now, his voice coming from inside of my head. *"Jacey can you hear me?"* I spoke out loud, expecting no sound to come out like when I was with Lucifer. There was a rush of relief when I heard my voice. "Yes" I smiled and shouted, "Yes!! I can hear you! Please help me! I—I don't know where I am... it's so dark and creepy and I can't see anything!" A sense of calm washed over me as Jesus spoke.

"Jacey, listen now, I want you to hold out your hand in front of you, okay? Hold it out and focus your life- force into the palm of your hand. You need to channel all of your power….. so concentrate hard okay?"

I did as instructed. Holding my hand in front of me I imagined colorful energy collecting in my body and envisioned it moving to my hand, my life-force burning in my palm. "Okay, I did it. Wh—What do I do now?" I waited for Jesus to answer, each second I was in the dark felt like an eternity.

"Ok, you need to create a portal just like the one Gideon created when he brought you home. Feel the energy, and as soon as you see the portal forming, envision yourself back at home.

Think as hard as you can because the portal will bring you wherever your thoughts are.."

Through gritted teeth, I strained my body directing all of my life-force in front of me until a tiny light shined and a spiraling portal took shape. "I'm doing it, I can see it!" I yelled out in excitement.

"Good, come home Jacey, it's time to wake up." Wake up? I made my way into the portal eager to escape the eerie feeling that lingered in the darkness and moved as fast as I could, slipping through to the other side.

The portal had brought me to my bedroom I looked down and saw myself laying in bed with Gideon and Jesus sitting at my bedside. My hands were transparent. *How'd I get in astral form?* Jesus looked up, "You need to get back in your body Jacey." I felt an electric shock go through me when I plugged into my physical body and with a gasp, I opened my eyes.

Oh my God. I tried to sit up but Gideon shushed me, pushing my shoulders back, forcing me to stay laying down. "Don't get up yet Love. You shouldn't strain yourself we still need to find out what happened." He looked scared to death. "I'm okay, don't worry— I know what happened." I shuddered remembering my encounter with Lucifer.

"You need to tell us what you remember Jacey." Jesus said. "No Angel has ever succumb to unconsciousness like that before. You were in an entire different realm outside this dimension! It's lucky there was still part of your life-force connected to your body for me to channel my thoughts through to you----otherwise…." Jesus stopped for a second and seemed to change his mind about what he would say, he looked at me, "What happened? What did you feel? Did you see anything? What do you remember?"

I sat there thinking for a moment. *Was any of it even real or just a bad reaction to the Well?* "All I know is that I *saw* Lucifer. Like, in *real life* I…. He had me in this room or cave--" I shook my head, it sounded crazy saying it out loud. "fire surrounded it and---it was so hot. He said there will be unimaginable horrors." I looked at Gideon and then at Jesus, "He's coming back *soon*." It was a choice not to tell them about the deal he offered me even though I knew I would not *take* it. A part of me felt like it would make me look bad, Jesus already said my heart had been touched by envy, the last thing I wanted was for them to think I was able to be swayed by evil.

I sat up and threw my feet over the side of the bed. "Whoa, whoa, whoa, easy Love." Gideon said. "How did *Lucifer* get to her— is that even possible?" he looked to Jesus, "I don't know. It's— Well, I thought it impossible for Lucifer to gain access to Heaven which was why he is using Damien to lead his army but perhaps things have changed." Jesus appeared as lost and confused as we were, he rubbed his forehead with his hand as he thought out loud of scenarios.

"He must have gained enough power to create his own portals and astral project his essence here? Perhaps Heavens shield is weakened that badly? But how can it be without our knowing? No. The only thing that makes sense is the portals."

He looked at us. "That must be how he got to Jacey. What I don't know... *is why.* Why would he go through all of that trouble to get to you and not just attack? It makes little sense but I'm glad you're alive."

I stood up. "When I drank from the Well, I saw him too. Well, his 'past' him. anyway, I thought I was crazy and imagining things but I swear-- he *looked* at me in one of my visions. Like, he *looked right at me."* Jesus looked puzzled.

"That's most definitely not possible there's no way he could see you--unless he knew you would be drinking from the well then he could send his consciousness back. But the connection and amount of power that would take--"

His voice trailed off and his eyes widened, he looked at Gideon and jumped to his feet. "I must meet with the Guardians and speak with Father." He had a look on his face that alarmed me.

"Something's wrong. There is something we're missing. It's *not right here.* You stay with Jacey at all times! Do not under any circumstance leave her we *cannot* afford another episode like this!"

Gideon nodded. "Be careful sir." Jesus went out to the patio and turned back to face us. "Begin Jacey's training as soon as possible I'll send Zahara and Maleki here to help with everything she needs. Be vigilant brother, we must be ready for any further attempts from Lucifer to get to her. He has a link with her and has taken an interest in her somehow and until we figure it out, we're helpless. We have precious little time. I will find out how to handle this—situation." He looked at both of us and nodded a final time before he disappeared.

CHAPTER TWENTY-ONE: ON THE RUN

Gideon looked onto the patio where Jesus had left and, as if a thought had occurred to him, turned grabbing my arms, pulling me close. My breath caught in my throat, our eyes locked and he stared, a deep, penetrating, soul searching stare at me sending jolts of electricity everywhere through my body.

The hair on my arms raised, covering me with goosebumps as he ran his hands over my shoulders, up and down my arms. “Jacey,” He held both of my hands in front of him and looked down at them. “I—I cannot even describe what I felt when I thought I'd lost you.” His eyes glistened, he inhaled. “I thought you'd never know how I felt about you and that I'd never have the chance to do *this.”* He leaned in and kissed me with a fiery passion I had never thought was possible.

His hands explored my body, and he rested them on my hips, squeezing the small of my back and pulling me closer to him as his soft lips caressed mine. I wrapped my arms around his neck kissing him back eagerly; all the love I had been fighting to keep locked away had its release, and it was a beautiful feeling. *I love you Gideon.*

No matter how hard I had tried to rationalize it, this pull I had always felt for Gideon was real. There was something about him, that drew me in more than looks, personality, or circumstance. Gideon was the other half to my whole, my soulmate, I never wanted to be without him, and he felt the same way.

We held onto each other, neither one of us wanting to let our moment go. His body was warm, strong, and I felt safe in his arms and every inch of my body longed for *more.* We fought back our passion and stopped with ragged breathing, looking at each other with new eyes; Gideon and I were in love.

"I love you Jacey... *so much,* I promise to protect you, I can't ever lose you again." *This feels like a dream.* "Gideon I---" I laughed out loud at myself in disbelief we had this conversation. "Well, I'm sure you already know this, but, I have been trying to convince myself that my feelings for you were impossible since I got here. I've loved you from the moment I met you." He hugged me and laughed. "Me to Love, me too."

We held each other for a moment longer until the reality of our dire situation crept back into my head. *How can we be together? We have a war coming….* I pushed myself back and looked at Gideon. "What's the matter love?" There was a lump in my throat, I swallowed hard and paced the floor as panic set in.

"How are we going to be together? A war is coming where we could lose our lives! And even if we win can we be together then I mean... is—is that allowed?" I couldn't imagine being around Gideon every day, in love with him, but not *with him.*

Gideon smiled that smile stopping me in my tracks. "Calm down and relax okay?" He walked over placing his hands on my shoulders. "We *can* be together Love; there are no rules against love here! They compose this place of love. We have no choice but to wait to be together; there is a war to fight and we must focus all of our energies on that. But I swear to you, we will *win* and when we do..." He lifted my chin with his finger and kissed my forehead. "We will have all the time in the world to spend together. Promise, Love." As he spoke, I laid my head on his chest and listened to his voice with a smile. Gideon loved me, we would be together after this war, I clung to that promise, for strength and courage.

My mind was on one thing right now, I pushed myself back to look at him. "Can we train now? Please, I want--" I shook my head, this wasn't a want, it was a necessity. "No, I *need* to learn everything." He chuckled, "Easy tiger. You'll start soon, but we need to wait for Maleki and Zahara--" Disappointment hit me like a truck. All I wanted was to defend myself but it seemed like there was *always* something hindering me from doing just that. Gideon looked at me and saw how upset I was and thought for a second.

"You know what? Come outside on the beach, I can show you a few things while we wait." I jumped up, running out onto the patio. "Don't you want to put your training clothes on first?" Gideon shouted still in the room. "Oh. Ha, I guess I got a little ahead of myself." I turned back around and ran back into my bedroom.

Gideon stepped out, closing the door behind him, "I'll wait for you in the living room, give you your privacy." I hurried and slipped out of my gown and hung it back up in my closet to put my training clothes on. The material was thick but light and stretched with every move of my body, I walked over to my mirror and put my hair up in a high bun, out of my face and checked myself out. *I look ready to kick some serious demon ass.*

When I stepped into the living room, I stretched my arms out with a little turn. "So what do you think?" Gideon nodded, "I think you look ready for your first lesson." We walked out onto the beach, Gideon opened his wings wide so I did the same and we began my first lesson.

"During battle, your reflexes should be intuitive: you should be able to block an attack and counter it without as much as a second thought." He blitzed at me and I froze. "Hit me!" He commanded, his request shocked me. "What? Like, hit you?!" He stood there, nodding. "Yes, hit me don't worry, you won't hurt me that is *if you can even touch me.*" He was taunting me now, trying to get me to come at him but I hesitated.

"I can't do this, I don't want to hit you." I said, frustrated.

"You must, this is how you learn." He put his hands up motioning me to come at him.

"There has to be other way though, can't you magically teach me without all of—this?"

"No," he scoffed, "There is NO other way, we've all been in your position before, you can do this. So stop thinking and start swinging, believe it or not, God made you for this, but you won't see that until you *try."*

"Okay," I nodded, "Let's do this."

With a grunt, I swung my arms, Gideon moved his head out of the way with ease calm and collected. He had grace and speed but I pressed forward, swinging again, fists flailing through the air. After several frustrating minutes, I was aggravated and disheartened. "This is impossible, I don't know how to fight! How can I learn if I can't even hit you?"

Gideon stifled a laugh, I glared at him. He cleared his throat, "You're holding back Love, you're not hitting me because you don't *want* to hit me." Holding his face inches from mine he asked, "Now, do you want to defend yourself and protect those who can't—or do you want to run in fear like a *coward?*" His tone was harsh, and I scowled at him. "I am NOT a coward! And no, I *don't want* to hit you! Why would I want to hurt you?"

With a smooth step back, he took a fighting stance again. "Hurting me should be the *last thing* on your mind right now! Do you think for a second the demons we will face in this war will take it easy on you? Don't be naïve! You need to learn how to defend yourself! When we train, we train as if we are trying to kill each other, not because we *want* to, but because that is what we are facing: An army with one sole purpose---to destroy every one of us! Now, if you won't fight me with everything you have then you leave me no choice but to force you."

He swung at me and I blocked him with my forearm, it was a reflex I never knew I had. "Atta girl—now fight me and hold *nothing* back!" Another blow came my way and connected hard, knocking me down to the ground. I shot back up to my feet furious. *He hit me! I can't believe he hit me!* I rubbed my face. *Why didn't it hurt?*

"It doesn't hurt because you feel no pain in Heaven. But trust me when I tell you, Lucifer's army *can and will hurt you.* So get up and take this seriously, it is your only chance to *learn*. Our goal is to be so fast, so strong, that even though his army wins by sheer size, we make-up for that in *skill.* You need these skills, you said it yourself that we have little time."

He's right. I took a deep breath and copied Gideons stance nodding at him I was ready, and we began. This time, I held nothing back, determined to move faster and hit harder. This wasn't about me versus him, this was about us versus Lucifer and I had to see it that way too. He came across with a blow to my face, I ducked my head down avoiding it and shot my fist into his abdomen as hard as I could. The force sent him flying backwards, he dug his feet into the beach and a cloud of sand flew into the air behind him. "That's more like it Love!"

We trained for hours, I learned how to block, hit, counter-attack and held nothing back. Every swing, every kick, was as if my life depended on it, Gideon praised me when I did good, and pushed me harder when I missed something, forcing me to push my limits. In one day, I had learned all the basic of hand to hand combat, and I was eager to learn more—*tomorrow*.

CHAPTER TWENTY-TWO: FIELD TRAINING

I hit the ground with a soft thud, it may not have hurt getting knocked down, but it sure bruised my ego. *I'll never learn.* "Ugh!!!" I growled. Gideon reached his hand down to help me up, and I ripped him to the ground with me and stole a kiss. His soft lips molded to mine making butterflies go crazy in my stomach. "Jacey--" Gideon said between my lips. "We *need* to concentrate. *You* need to concentrate!" He pushed me away from him and looked at me.

Stopping my playful flirtation, I looked away feeling embarrassed. "Maybe I'm not the best trainer for you, we *both* distract one another and I can't help you like this, Love." He motioned to us laying on the beach tangled up, and dropped his hand in frustration. I stood up dusting the sand off of my body and reached down to help him.

"No, you cannot." Zahara said with disapproval clear in her tone. I jumped and Gideon shot up to his feet flustered. "Zahara!

Maleki! Glad to see you've finally made it!" They stared at us for a moment before Zahara spoke, "We had *business* to attend to first—other orders. I see you two have become — comfortable with each other. A little too *close* for a trainer though." She noted.

Gideon cleared his throat and shifted his feet, "We um—we're just finishing up here, Jacey has developed her skills after just one session—It's rather impress--"

Maleki scoffed, putting his hand up, cutting him off. *Rude.* "Do you take us for fools Gideon? We saw you two, rolling around with your love session moments ago! You call *that* training? What purpose does your role to her serve if you both find yourselves dead in battle because of this foolishness? Or worse—captured? Are you willing to risk that?" He was chastising Gideon, and it wasn't fair he was trying to train me.

I put my hands up, "Please stop yelling at him, he's been a great trainer. I was the one playing around so if you want to yell at someone, yell at me!" Gideon held his hand up for me to stop talking, "Jacey, you don't have to say anything, they're right, I manage your training, it's my duty--"

"NOT anymore!" Zahara and Maleki said in sync. My jaw dropped open. Gideon stood there, acquiescent; he did not object. I was angry that Gideon got in trouble for my stupidity, and angry that Zahara and Maleki thought they could tell us anything. "You're right." Gideon said.

Why does he sound so happy about this? Maybe he doesn't want to train me anymore. He gave me a sideways look, and I averted my eyes embarrassed that he was reading my self loathing thoughts. "What I mean is--" he continued, "What we need to be doing is field training, being alone…. here, it's just too relaxed of an environment. Field training will give Jacey everything she needs: accountability, atmosphere, and competition. Give me one week of field training with all of us together, and I guarantee she will be war-ready." He gave me a side smile and a wink.

I subdued the smirk on my face as best as I could and looked at Zahara and Maleki. They looked at one another and sighed, "One week." Maleki said, and Gideon nodded. "We'll do this together, no more of this--" she waved her hand gesturing to Gideon and I, "Nonsense! We have too much work to do and there are too many lives at stake. You can gallivant around on your own time but training sessions are to remain strictly professional." Her thick braid swung around as she turned with Maleki and walked back into my house. *They're staying?*

"Jesus sent them here to help watch out for you Jacey. We need all the help and protection we can get and besides—they're our *friends.*" Gideon chuckled *"They didn't seem friendly from where I was standing!"* I grumbled under my breath. He placed both hands on my shoulders, and looked me in the eye, grinning. "Relax! They want what's best for you, what's best for all of us. I told you we distracted to each other! We *both* know it, but I can't help myself; I just love you so much!"

He scooped me up, swinging me around in his arms and I relaxed. "I love you too!" I sighed content. *He's right. They want what's best, we are all in this together and they must be just as scared as I am.* I held Gideons hand as we walked up the steps and into my house to join Zahara and Maleki.

They were sitting at the dining room table talking to each other and looked up at us as we stepped inside. I felt bad for getting angry with them earlier; they had only done what Jesus told them to. “I have an extra bedroom if you want privacy or to sleep or anything.” I said hoping to make them feel welcomed and at ease.

Zahara smiled at me and Maleki nodded, “You're kind, but a bedroom won't be necessary, we must remain vigilant in case of another episode--” he looked at me for a long moment. “What happened? Do you have any recollection of this—Lucifer incident?” A sharp chill went down my spine at the mention of *him.* “I—well, I was standing right there in the kitchen headed to the table with my tea and--” My palms felt clammy and it became hard to breath recalling the horrible experience. *Get it together and tell them what happened.* I commanded myself and collected my thoughts.

“These visions came in flashes in my mind like when I had drank from the Well except for this time, I was awake and in my body—or at least I thought I was.” I was gesturing with my hands as I spoke trying to paint a picture for them as detailed as possible. “Then everything blurred out, and I heard this deafening ringing in my ears. It was *painful* like a sharp, stabbing pain going through my skull, crippling me, I saw Gideon step towards me then disappear as my house crumbled in flames.”

Gideon held my hand and spoke, “She convulsed and by the time I had reached her to catch her from falling, she was unconscious, and unresponsive. I have seen nothing like it... ever.” I shuddered. “It was a traumatic experience. When I realized I wasn’t in Heaven anymore, I tried to find a way out. But *He* was there — Lucifer. Toying with me, threatening of what was to come he told me to leave Heaven and get Gideon to leave too, that it was a deal just for me because he didn’t want me to get *hurt*.”

Gideon looked at me perplexed. “You never told me that.” I smiled at him. “It didn’t seem important at the time — Because I would NEVER make a deal with the devil to turn my back on my family, and my duty. This is my destiny, and that's what I told Lucifer when I declined his so called offer.” Zahara laughed, “Oh... I bet he didn’t like that answer too much.”

I shook my head and raised my eyebrows. “No, he didn’t. But before he sent me into the darkness, he said ‘See you soon’ like he would be seeing me again or something. And that’s the last thing I remember, I woke up and was in a creepy dark place, I could hear Gideon telling me to wake up, but I *was* awake, or at least my conscious was then I heard Jesus’ voice and came back through a portal.” I looked around at everyone staring at me and bit my lip, “And well,--here I am.”

Maleki got up from the table and walked towards me holding his hands up to my head, “May I?” I nodded. “Be my guest, maybe you can see what happened better than I can.” *I hope you can.* I wanted nothing more than to figure out *how* Lucifer was able to get me so we could stop him from ever doing it again.

CHAPTER TWENTY-THREE: SEEING IS BELIEVING

I watched as Maleki's large eyes became blank, as if he were looking at something far away. The galactic swirls seemed to freeze for a moment as he focused and I *felt him plug into my consciousness.* I completely knew of his presence in my mind. *This feels funny.* Maleki was silent in front of me and silent inside of my head too. *Is it working? Can you see anything? What do you see?* "Shhh" He shushed me.

I tried to stop thinking and focused on Maleki's rhythmic breathing. I wanted him to tell me something, anything about my incident so we could have an advantage of any kind. From where I was standing, Lucifer had a lot going for him. The element of surprise, unknown powers, an immeasurable army and he had found a weak link in Heaven…. me.

We all stood perfectly still afraid to even breathe while Maleki was looking around inside of my head. *Please find something that can help.* Time seemed to drag on forever standing there, but I waited desperate for answers. Maleki stood like a statue, his only movement came from his breathing. His eyes became clear, and he lowered his hands from my head looking at me with a sympathy in his eyes. "Oh you poor thing, you've been through a lot since you ascended haven't you?"

His words triggered something in me and caused tears to well up and overflow. I'd been so busy trying to deal with what I was feeling and compartmentalizing my emotions the weight of stress was crushing me inside. My throat tightened as I cried in silence, afraid that if I spoke, I would lose what little control I had left.

Zahara and Gideon stepped closer and Maleki wrapped his huge arms around all three of us. After a moment Gideon asked what was preying on all of our minds. "Did you see anything that could help us? Any clue how this happened?" Maleki shook his head, "No, I saw only what she went through, with a glimpse of what she saw is to come. The attack *will* happen, and soon but as far as Lucifer's ability to get to Jacey--" He looked at me. "He seemed to connect with her consciousness—a part of her life force—and I don't have the slightest idea how that's even possible."

"I do." A familiar voice said, we all turned to see Jesus standing in the doorway. "You're back!" I said as I ran and hugged him. "What did you find out?" Zahara asked stepping forward embracing him for a long moment. Jesus looked dejected. "Come, let us sit down for a moment." He motioned to the living room, and we all filed in taking a seat on my couches.

Jesus sighed. "We have a problem… well, a couple—but one regarding *you*." He looked distressed as he spoke the words. "The reason Lucifer can connect with your consciousness like he never has before is through Damien." It made little sense. *How does Damien have a power to infiltrate consciousness?*

"How is that possible? What's Damien have to do Jacey?" Gideon asked.

"I don't understand, does he have a power we don't know about?" Zahara asked.

Maleki raised his hands up to hush everyone, ending the time for questions, "We all want to know what Jesus has found out, please, let him speak and tell us what he knows. Then we can ask all the questions we want."

Jesus nodded at Maleki, "Thank you."

Maleki bowed his head, "You're welcome sir, please continue."

Jesus scanned all of our faces. "Damien has a unique connection with Jacey he's--" he paused. "He's your brother Jacey."

I scoffed, then laughed thinking this must be a sick joke. *I don't have a brother.* "You're kidding right?" Jesus looked like he felt sorry for me, he believed what he'd just said. "This is crazy you guys, I'm an only child my mom called me her 'miracle baby' my entire life." I looked around at my friends shocked faces. *They think it's true.* "I can't believe you'd even think, *that monsters offspring is my brother!"* Gideon rubbed my back, "Calm down, love."

I jumped up shaking him off of me. "No, I WILL NOT CALM DOWN! IT'S A LIE!" I stood in my living room yelling. "I don't believe it! And you shouldn't because it's bullshit!" I clasped my hand over my mouth looking at Jesus ashamed. Tears welled up in my eyes, an anguished sob erupted from my throat as I ran to my bedroom. *You can all just leave me alone since you think I'm related to the Devil!*

I slammed the door hard behind me and collapsed to the floor, leaning against it to prevent anyone from following. *It isn't true, it isn't true, it isn't true!* I held my hands on both sides of my head, refusing to think any more and wiped the tears off my face crawling across the floor up into my bed. Tired of being awake, and tired of dealing with everything, I forced my eyes shut counting the tears that fell off of my cheek until I was asleep. I wanted to escape this reality even if it was for a fleeting moment.

CHAPTER TWENTY-FOUR: NO ESCAPE

I awoke kicking the covers off of me; my body was sweltering. I sat up and swung my legs over the side of the bed. I felt groggy and drained from the heat. *Why is it so hot?* "Gideon? Jesus? Are you guys still out there?" I called out down the hall. *How long have I been out?* I continued down the hall and into the living room.

"Hello? Zahara?----Is anyone here?" There was a sigh from behind me, "I thought you'd never ask…." That voice was familiar — *Lucifer!* Prepared to defend myself, I whirled around in a fighting stance but he stood there, leaning up against the wall in the hallway, a sinister smile plastered on his face. "Surprise!" His long fingers wiggled in the air as if in celebration, his happiness disgusted me. "Long time no see sweet Jacey... glad you made it back *safe* from limbo..." His tone was tranquil and casual.

What do you want? I glared hard at him. "*I* must confess---It surprised me to find you're still *here*… after I was *generous enough* to offer you your freedom without consequence. Tsk-tsk." He shook his finger at me and I glared back. "You shouldn't test my patience child. I'm offering you, a *kindness.* We are *family you know*." That did it for me, I was furious. "Don't give me that, I'm no family to you!" I spat, "And I don't want your *deal* or *anything* to do with *you.* Your lies don't deceive me and I'm not going *anywhere*!"

We locked in a staring contest and I prayed my face showed Lucifer the abhorrence for him that filled me. "Leave me! I would rather die fighting you than live a second of my life knowing I helped *you.*" My sternness infuriated him and I watched his face grow enraged. "YOU INSOLENT GIRL! HOW DARE YOU?" I swallowed hard but did not falter, fighting my fear. *I will stand my ground.*

In an instant he was in front of me panting with anger expelling his hot breath all over my face, he picked me up by my shoulders, I broke free with a quick slam of my arms onto his elbows; a little trick Gideon had taught me. I felt a moment of satisfaction as he turned to walk away before his back-hand sent me flying across my living room. My back slammed into my bookcase, and I winced in pain as I stood up. *Gideon was right, they can hurt us.* I stood up straight, ready to fight.

Lucifer rushed grabbing my throat, lifting me up with one hand then he dug his black nails into the skin on my shoulder, dragging them down my arm, tearing my flesh. I screamed in agony as I felt the venom enter my body. It burned like a thousand fire ants were feasting inside of me, my veins turning black as it spread. The pain was unbearable I couldn't help but scream, it was becoming more intense as each second passed.

"I could *end* you, make no mistake you foolish child! This--" He lifted his fingers showcasing the nails dripping with my blood, "Is *nothing* compared to what's coming for ALL THE Angels in Heaven! Stay and die, or leave — *and live."* He dropped me to the floor writhing in agony and gasping for air. "GO—BACK—TO--" I panted breathless "HELL!" I screamed with all my air in my lungs.

A cry escaped me as Lucifer rushed me hard, kicking me in the ribs and I heard a loud "CRACK!" followed by intense pain in my side. He lifted me high above his head and slammed me into the floor I felt panic set in as I realized my life was at the mercy of a merciless demon. "That's enough Father!" Someone said; I had never heard this voice before. *He called him 'father'...* There was only one person who would call him father. I pulled myself up, holding my side; It felt like every bone in my body was broke and the venom was making everything around me come in and out of focus. But I wanted to see him, I had to see him for myself.

I broke down as my eyes focused on Damien. It was undeniable, he looked like my *mother... like me.* The only difference was that like his father, he had alabaster white hair. "Stick to the plan, father." Damien said through gritted teeth. "Remember your *tone* Boy! I *know* what the plan is; *I* am the one who *made* it!" Lucifer retorted.

He grabbed my face, lifting my weak head up. "Our sweet Jacey here is not cooperating, I'm giving her a little *motivation*." I was having trouble breathing and staying conscious, the only thing that helped me was focusing on the pain from the venom that was killing me. My breathing was shallow as I tried to minimize the pain of my broken ribs.

"Oh," Damien pursed his lips, "Please, forgive my father sis, he can get a little—passionate." Damien approached my side and threw my arm over his shoulders I winced from the pain too weak to stop him. "No, no—don't—*touch me."* I garbled my words and slipped into unconsciousness. "Don't worry sis, you'll come around... you have to, believe me, I don't *want* to kill you—but I will..." I heard Damien's voice echo through my mind he continued talking but nothing else he said was clear.

CHAPTER TWENTY-FIVE: THE HEALING PROCESS

I could hear indistinct voices as I came to feeling weak and dizzy, I opened my eyes and blinked a few times, trying to get my blurry surroundings to come into focus. "Where am I?" My body had warm tingles and Zahara was kneeling over the couch with her hands glowing Jade and Amber light over my body. Gideon, Jesus, and Maleki were standing close by watching Zahara heal me. It was incredible I could feel her powers radiating in and around me, the relief was indescribable.

My broken ribs and the burning pain of Lucifer's poison eased up and I watched the scratches he'd left on my arm disappear, the black ink that stained my veins receded until my skin looked clear again and the burning stopped. "Wow---thank you so much." Gideon's face shown worry.

"Are you certain you got it all, there's no trace of it left? You're certain right?" He placed his hand over my forehead and looked into my eyes, I reached my hand up touching the side of his face. *I'm fine, I promise.*

"She's healed, and one-hundred percent venom free." Zahara said.

Not completely….. I still need to recover from the fact I have the spawn of Satan for a brother.. She stood up and looked down at me raising her eyebrows, "Sorry, I can't help you with that kind of healing--" she crouched down next to me, holding my hand "And I'm here for you if you ever want to talk about it. But we need to know what happened because one minute you're here, the next, you're gone! Then you turn up hours later to the point of ascending." her eyes widened, "You're lucky we got to you when we did, a few more minutes, and I wouldn't have been able to heal you. Where did you go, what happened?" I gave her a confused look, I had gone nowhere.

"What? I didn't disappear you guys did. Lucifer attacked me right here. I went in my room to force myself to fall asleep—I needed a break from thinking, when I woke up--- I walked around looking for you guys. No one was here though. Well no one except Lucifer---" I stopped myself and looked at Zahara. "Look, I was here the whole time." Gideon helped me to sit up then sat beside me. "We've gone nowhere, you disappeared. When you went into your room, we gave you a few minutes to cool down, then I went to talk to you, but you were gone." I looked down, frustrated by yet another mystery.

He dipped his head lower, looking me in the eye. "We looked for you for hours all over Heaven thinking maybe you left the house when we couldn't find you, we came back and you were in your bed laid out — as if you were—you were almost--" His eyes were glowing an intense blue and he shook with rage. "He'll pay for what he did to you."

Jesus placed a hand on Gideons shoulder. "Calm yourself brother, our time will come. You can't be surprised he did that to her, this is Lucifer we're talking about. But why wouldn't he kill her?" he looked at me, "Not that I'm not thankful you're alive because I am. I don't know what he could gain from these moments of stolen time with Jacey though." No one had an answer for that.

One detail still bothered me, "Lucifer, and I fought right here." shaking my hand towards the bookcase, "He smashed that thing to bits with my body! Throwing me around in this room, he almost killed me he would have until—it doesn't matter."

I stopped myself from finishing not wanting to give Damien any credit for saving my life. "Until what?" Gideon prodded.

"Well, Lucifer was about to kill me but he stopped—Damien told him to stop. He said they needed to 'stick to the plan'" I whispered.

Gideon stiffened at the revelation. "You saw Damien?" He looked at Jesus who shared the same expression of shock and worry, "Here, in Heaven?" He said again.

I nodded. "Yes, he was here in this room." I stopped speaking and felt sick. There was no other feeling to have when you're tied to Lucifer via a brother you didn't even know you had. I shivered just thinking about it; the time for war was no longer a mere prophecy; the time for war was upon us.

I thought about what Jesus had said earlier and something inside clicked and I got it, I knew what they could gain and what this was all about. *Stolen time….* "That's it, I think I know what their plan is!" I exclaimed, jumping to my feet. "Jesus, you said something about stolen time before... and that got me thinking…"

I paced the floor with excitement. "I know we are on the precipice of the war... I can feel it. Lucifer is both hindering my ability to train and stealing our time. Don't you see? In Lucifer's original conversation with me, he told me to leave, he knew I would refuse, but that's not why he took me; he took me so you'd go digging for answers to find out how, knowing you'd uncover the truth about Damien. He caused a distraction, it has worked us up in a frenzy ever since the first incident."

Everyone looked at me lost. "Don't you see? THAT'S THE PLAN! It is a distraction. While they preoccupy the enemy—we're vulnerable, Lucifer is trying to gain the advantage on as many fields as possible, me never being trained as a Healing Angel is his best option since he failed at preventing my ascension!"

I was panting, pacing the floor with excitement. "He doesn't want me, but he doesn't want me to save any of the Angels when we face each other either… He wants to make sure we don't survive." I stood there, waiting for someone to say something or share in my excitement but no one moved, they contemplated my dissection of Lucifer's motives.

Jesus' eyes narrowed, "It has distracted us—you make a good point, but I still feel there's more to it than hindering our training." He shook his head and sighed. "We can't waste another second if that's his plan, we need to train you and not waste another second on Lucifer and Damien's games."

Jesus stood up, "Round the clock field training begins now, you have so much to learn and little time to do it." I shrieked with excitement. "Yes! I'm so ready to get started! Just wait, Lucifer thinks he has it all figured out, he thinks he has us where he wants us, I want to see the look on his smug face when we face annihilation, and defeat them!" It pumped me and I felt proud of myself; Instead of fearing Lucifer's wrath, I was ready to face it, and overcome it alongside my brothers and sisters.

As far as Damien went, I would never uncover the truth about our relationship—or how it was even possible, I had to accept it, and move on. I couldn't, and wouldn't allow my emotions to hinder my training a second longer; doing so would put us all at risk.

We followed Jesus out onto my patio, Gideon hugged me and I held onto him and pressed my face into his chest, breathing in; he had his own smell that was sweet and woodsy. My love for him was enough for me to overcome anything, and I looked forward to winning this war, so we would have an eternity to spend together.

He looked at me his eyes full of the devotion and love I felt for him. *How did I get so lucky?* His curly hair hung on his forehead covering his brows and he gave me his classic side smile and wink. “Let's go!” Jesus ordered, and we took to the sky, heading to the training field. *I'm ready.*

CHAPTER TWENTY-SIX: NO MORE GAMES

Time was of the essence, we flew as fast as our wings could take us. The pressure was on each of us to ensure we could to take on Damien and Lucifer's army when they attacked and I wondered how many more times they would take me before that day came.

Training was the most pressing matter at hand because I needed to learn to heal *and* fight and do it fast. The only way that could happen would be to stop trying to discern Lucifer's plan and focus on defeating him. Thinking about the war reminded me of my visions and what we were expecting from Damien and Lucifer and I wondered what they were doing with all the cylinders they trapped the ascending Angels in.

There were more questions than answers and it frustrated me, Jesus hung back to talk. "You know, we don't always need all the answers Jacey, sometimes, one must learn to go on faith. Faith it will be all right, even if it isn't, what's meant to be will be." He looked at me with loving eyes. "You needn't worry, it is *my place* to worry about each of you and my *duty* to protect and defend Heaven when Father can't. I couldn't do it without you, each of you are special and necessary, we will overcome this... together. Have faith, and you'll see."

Although he seemed confident in us, I doubted if we would come out of this war unscathed. My heart sunk at the thought of what our loss would mean for the universe—and for God. Jesus said it was 'his duty to protect Heaven when God couldn't' the context of that statement was clear: God was incapable of defending Heaven now and I wondered how bad off he was.

We approached the field, and I saw the other Angels training already. It hit me with a rush of excitement as we made our descent. "Angels!" Jesus shouted as he landed and everyone gathered round. I recognized Ashira, and Colin in the crowd and waved at them. Grateful for the opportunity to contribute to protecting Heaven.

Jesus stood in the middle of the field as each group of Angels waited for orders. "As you all know, Jacey is our newest recruit, she has missed her training due to some--" He paused, "unforeseen circumstances and we are running out of time. The war is coming, and we must all be ready. Angels, we will train our sister for as long as it takes until she masters her offensive and defensive abilities."

Jesus paced back and forth as he spoke. "That means we will no longer be taking our evenings for ourselves, instead we will take shifts in training round the clock. I will assign Angels to stand watch at the ascension portal, Eden, and Paradise Valley to give ourselves as much time as possible to prepare for the attack. They have the element of surprise—we cannot afford to give them that, and we won't!"

The Angels nodded as Jesus pulled two of each group aside and assigned their posts. They would take the first shift to stand watch. I looked on in silence waiting for Jesus to instruct me on my first field lesson.

"Jacey, I want you to watch each group of Angels for a while, Zahara will stand with you and teach you how to heal at your next opportunity. Healing is the most significant thing for you to learn—It will take some time to embrace and master your gift and how we fight, we focus on our speed, reflexes, and strength and you must learn to master all." I nodded, determination on my face. *This is it.* I was ready for my first lesson.

Jesus clapped his hands together making a thunderous noise. "Angels, BEGIN!" I looked on from the sidelines with Zahara as the groups broke off and the training began. They were fast and attacked each other full force. The Arsenal Angels were creating swords, bows, and spears that shot across the sky like lightning bolts targeting their opposing group.

They were practicing with the Messenger Angels who moved at such speed that their bodies blurred out both on the ground and in the sky. "Wow—they go hard…" I said somewhat shocked watching the amount of pressure the Angels put on one another. Zahara laughed at my expression. "Well, you know

Damien will not be an easy adversary, we must train in the same manner we plan to fight; holding nothing back." I shook my head, "You sound like--"

As I spoke the words, I stopped, horrified to see Colin, the boyish little Messenger shot down from the sky by one of the silver lightning spears of the Arsenals. "Oh my God! Colin!" I screamed, Zahara grabbed my hand, "Oh your first heal! Yay! Come on!" She pulled as we rushed over to where Colin lay on the ground.

No one cares? The Angels around continued their training as if nothing happened with no concern, their faces shown only cold determination. I dropped to my knees but Colin smiled and had a calm expression. Zahara kneeled next to me, "Remove the arrow--" she instructed, excitement danced around her eyes.

I held my hand on Colin's chest with wide eyes and he laughed. "It's okay, it doesn't even hurt! I can take it out for you!" He reached for the arrow. "No!" Zahara stopped his hand and looked at me. "You must do as I say! Don't hesitate, you are here to help. Now... remove the arrow!" I nodded and took a breath. "Okay…." I placed a hand on his chest again, and pulled the arrow out, throwing it to the side.

Zahara grabbed my hands and held them over the small wound right above his heart and I could feel my life force pulsating through my chest and arms to my palms. A small glow shown and Zahara smiled and nodded, "Yes! There you go, *feel* the power of your gift and *Heal* him." I channeled my life force and watched as the wound disappeared.

My hands felt warm, I wiggled my fingers and laughed as Colin jumped back up, "Good as new," He dusted himself off and gave me a two-fingered salute, "Thanks! See ya later!" He disappeared back into the crowd, zipping through the Angels taking their weapons and knocking them down as he caught them off guard.

Zahara and I stood up, I looked down at my hands pumping them, "Can you believe it? Because I can't believe it, that was amazing!" I said as she chuckled, "Yes! I told you it was easy, almost instinctual—we just have to work on your speed and nerves!" she elbowed me in the side. "Well, I didn't want to hurt him!" She shook her head and wrapped her arm around me, "Silly girl. We don't hurt—we only help!" And we both walked back to the sideline of the field to wait for more Angels to heal.

After a few more chances to work on my healing, I found that it was easier and more efficient each time. The Angels hurt each other a lot more than I expected, but that was a blessing because I needed as much practice as I could get.

Jesus broke off from the Warrior Angels he was training with and approached us. *Uh-oh. It's time.* I smiled even though I felt like I was about to be a fish in a shark tank. He looked at Zahara, "Is she ready? Has she healed enough?" Zahara nodded. "She's a natural — it took little to no instruction, she's ready." She bumped me with her shoulder, "Healing is the easy part, now it's time for you to learn how to fight!"

I slapped my hands against my thighs, "Okay, let's do it! Just tell me where you want me." Jesus scanned the groups, I thought he was looking to put me in the easiest group first which would have been the Elemental Angels. But he looked over them and pointed to the Warrior Angels. "Go with the Gideon and the other Warriors, they'll get you off on the right foot." Thinking about training with Gideon again made my stomach fill with butterflies and I grinned.

Jesus and Zahara walked me over, and Gideon flew down, landing in front of us. We smiled at each other and he nodded to Jesus. *Silent speaking, huh?* Jesus patted my back. "It's time for you to fight Jacey. This will be hard for you—trust me, it was hard for every Angel at first. But it's something you must do."

"She'll be war ready when the time comes, sir." Gideon assured. Zahara turned to leave with Jesus and I chased after her, grabbing her arm, "Aren't you staying with me?" She shook her head, smiling. "No, you don't need me in the way, The Warriors can take it from here, besides, I need to go speak with the Arsenals about something." She gave me a warm hug and whispered in my ear, *"You're a natural, just believe in yourself, in your ability—you got this!"* She was right, if I ever expected to face this war, I needed to know I could go it alone if I had to.

Gideon took a wide offensive stance in front of me, and I copied it. "Good, you remember, now just like before—try to hit me," he winked. I gave it all I had; I swung, kicked, punched, and failed hundreds of times over. Gideon maneuvered around me, evading every attack I attempted with frustrating perfection. "This is useless! I can't even hit you once! How am I ever going to defend myself during the attack?" I griped, but this time, he did not stop instead, he came at me again with an overhand swing. I blocked it with my forearm and pushed him back angrily.

"Awe, don't be mad Love, it's called *training* for a reason, we help each other get better so we can all be ready—and you will be too." His words did nothing to calm the hurricane of emotions I held inside it was just too much too soon and it felt like I could never be as good or as fast as everyone else. In my mind, I had already lost the battle with Lucifer, I was just the weakest link still, Healer or not. He looked at me for a moment and then his face lit up, "I know what you need—follow me." He said as he flew up into the sky.

Time was of the essence, we flew as fast as our wings could take us. The pressure was on each of us to ensure we could to take on Damien and Lucifer's army when they attacked and I wondered how many more times they would take me before that day came.

Training was the most pressing matter at hand because I needed to learn to heal *and* fight and do it fast. The only way that could happen would be to stop trying to discern Lucifer's plan and focus on defeating him. Thinking about the war reminded me of my visions and what we were expecting from Damien and Lucifer and I wondered what they were doing with all the cylinders they trapped the ascending Angels in.

There were more questions than answers and it frustrated me, Jesus hung back to talk. "You know, we don't always need all the answers Jacey, sometimes, one must learn to go on faith. Faith it will be all right, even if it isn't, what's meant to be will be." He looked at me with loving eyes. "You needn't worry, it is *my place* to worry about each of you and my *duty* to protect and defend Heaven when Father can't. I couldn't do it without you, each of you are special and necessary, we will overcome this... together. Have faith, and you'll see."

Although he seemed confident in us, I doubted if we would come out of this war unscathed. My heart sunk at the thought of what our loss would mean for the universe—and for God. Jesus said it was 'his duty to protect Heaven when God couldn't' the context of that statement was clear: God was incapable of defending Heaven now and I wondered how bad off he was.

We approached the field, and I saw the other Angels training already. It hit me with a rush of excitement as we made our descent. "Angels!" Jesus shouted as he landed and everyone gathered round. I recognized Ashira, and Colin in the crowd and waved at them. Grateful for the opportunity to contribute to protecting Heaven.

Jesus stood in the middle of the field as each group of Angels waited for orders. "As you all know, Jacey is our newest recruit, she has missed her training due to some--" He paused, "unforeseen circumstances and we are running out of time. The war is coming, and we must all be ready. Angels, we will train our sister for as long as it takes until she masters her offensive and defensive abilities."

Jesus paced back and forth as he spoke. "That means we will no longer be taking our evenings for ourselves, instead we will take shifts in training round the clock. I will assign Angels to stand watch at the ascension portal, Eden, and Paradise Valley to give ourselves as much time as possible to prepare for the attack. They have the element of surprise—we cannot afford to give them that, and we won't!"

The Angels nodded as Jesus pulled two of each group aside and assigned their posts. They would take the first shift to stand watch. I looked on in silence waiting for Jesus to instruct me on my first field lesson.

"Jacey, I want you to watch each group of Angels for a while, Zahara will stand with you and teach you how to heal at your next opportunity. Healing is the most significant thing for you to learn—It will take some time to embrace and master your gift and how we fight, we focus on our speed, reflexes, and strength and you must learn to master all." I nodded, determination on my face. *This is it.* I was ready for my first lesson.

Jesus clapped his hands together making a thunderous noise. "Angels, BEGIN!" I looked on from the sidelines with Zahara as the groups broke off and the training began. They were fast and attacked each other full force. The Arsenal Angels were creating swords, bows, and spears that shot across the sky like lightning bolts targeting their opposing group.

They were practicing with the Messenger Angels who moved at such speed that their bodies blurred out both on the ground and in the sky. “Wow—they go hard…” I said somewhat shocked watching the amount of pressure the Angels put on one another. Zahara laughed at my expression. “Well, you know Damien will not be an easy adversary, we must train in the same manner we plan to fight; holding nothing back.” I shook my head, “You sound like--”

As I spoke the words, I stopped, horrified to see Colin, the boyish little Messenger shot down from the sky by one of the silver lightning spears of the Arsenals. “Oh my God! Colin!” I screamed, Zahara grabbed my hand, “Oh your first heal! Yay! Come on!” She pulled as we rushed over to where Colin lay on the ground.

No one cares? The Angels around continued their training as if nothing happened with no concern, their faces shown only cold determination. I dropped to my knees but Colin smiled and had a calm expression. Zahara kneeled next to me, “Remove the arrow--” she instructed, excitement danced around her eyes.

I held my hand on Colin’s chest with wide eyes and he laughed. “It’s okay, it doesn’t even hurt! I can take it out for you!” He reached for the arrow. “No!” Zahara stopped his hand and looked at me. “You must do as I say! Don't hesitate, you are here to help. Now... remove the arrow!” I nodded and took a breath. “Okay….” I placed a hand on his chest again, and pulled the arrow out, throwing it to the side.

Zahara grabbed my hands and held them over the small wound right above his heart and I could feel my life force pulsating through my chest and arms to my palms. A small glow shown and Zahara smiled and nodded, "Yes! There you go, *feel* the power of your gift and *Heal* him." I channeled my life force and watched as the wound disappeared.

My hands felt warm, I wiggled my fingers and laughed as Colin jumped back up, "Good as new," He dusted himself off and gave me a two-fingered salute, "Thanks! See ya later!" He disappeared back into the crowd, zipping through the Angels taking their weapons and knocking them down as he caught them off guard.

Zahara and I stood up, I looked down at my hands pumping them, "Can you believe it? Because I can't believe it, that was amazing!" I said as she chuckled, "Yes! I told you it was easy, almost instinctual—we just have to work on your speed and nerves!" she elbowed me in the side. "Well, I didn't want to hurt him!" She shook her head and wrapped her arm around me, "Silly girl. We don't hurt—we only help!" And we both walked back to the sideline of the field to wait for more Angels to heal.

After a few more chances to work on my healing, I found that it was easier and more efficient each time. The Angels hurt each other a lot more than I expected, but that was a blessing because I needed as much practice as I could get.

Jesus broke off from the Warrior Angels he was training with and approached us. *Uh-oh. It's time.* I smiled even though I felt like I was about to be a fish in a shark tank. He looked at Zahara, “Is she ready? Has she healed enough?” Zahara nodded. “She’s a natural — it took little to no instruction, she’s ready.” She bumped me with her shoulder, “Healing is the easy part, now it’s time for you to learn how to fight!”

I slapped my hands against my thighs, “Okay, let’s do it! Just tell me where you want me.” Jesus scanned the groups, I thought he was looking to put me in the easiest group first which would have been the Elemental Angels. But he looked over them and pointed to the Warrior Angels. “Go with the Gideon and the other Warriors, they’ll get you off on the right foot.” Thinking about training with Gideon again made my stomach fill with butterflies and I grinned.

Jesus and Zahara walked me over, and Gideon flew down, landing in front of us. We smiled at each other and he nodded to Jesus. *Silent speaking, huh?* Jesus patted my back. “It’s time for you to fight Jacey. This will be hard for you—trust me, it was hard for every Angel at first. But it's something you must do.”

“She’ll be war ready when the time comes, sir.” Gideon assured. Zahara turned to leave with Jesus and I chased after her, grabbing her arm, “Aren't you staying with me?” She shook her head, smiling. “No, you don’t need me in the way, The Warriors can take it from here, besides, I need to go speak with the Arsenals about something.” She gave me a warm hug and whispered in my ear, *“You’re a natural, just believe in yourself, in your ability—you got this!"* She was right, if I ever expected to face this war, I needed to know I could go it alone if I had to.

Gideon took a wide offensive stance in front of me, and I copied it. "Good, you remember, now just like before—try to hit me," he winked. I gave it all I had; I swung, kicked, punched, and failed hundreds of times over. Gideon maneuvered around me, evading every attack I attempted with frustrating perfection. "This is useless! I can't even hit you once! How am I ever going to defend myself during the attack?" I griped, but this time, he did not stop instead, he came at me again with an overhand swing. I blocked it with my forearm and pushed him back angrily.

"Awe, don't be mad Love, it's called *training* for a reason, we help each other get better so we can all be ready—and you will be too." His words did nothing to calm the hurricane of emotions I held inside it was just too much too soon and it felt like I could never be as good or as fast as everyone else. In my mind, I had already lost the battle with Lucifer, I was just the weakest link still, Healer or not. He looked at me for a moment and then his face lit up, "I know what you need—follow me." He said as he flew up into the sky.

CHAPTER TWENTY-SEVEN: THE JADE KATANA

When we got in the air, he searched the field below us. "Down there—let's go see Eliza and the Arsenal Angels."

"Why?" He gave me a side smile, "Well, to get you a weapon beautiful." *Hm. Beautiful, I could get used to that.* He laughed, pulling me down to the southern part of the field where Eliza and the other Arsenals were going full force against the Elementals.

Eliza turned and looked surprised to see us as she broke out of a fight and came over wiping her brow, "Phew! I'll tell you—Ashira runs a tough group!" I looked behind her watching as the battle continued. There were Angels flying in all directions as the Elementals threw the rocky turf and wind in every direction, causing chaos among the Arsenals as they created and shot their weapons back at them.

Each Angel moved with precision and purpose, none of them doubted their ability from what I could see and I envied them for their role in God's Army. Being a Healing Angel was hard, and sometimes lonely. I didn't have a large group to count on—it was just Zahara and I. And my gift was not for fighting, but for healing.

"So what can I do ya for?" Eliza asked.

Gideon cleared his throat, "Jacey is experiencing--" He looked at me, then back to Eliza. "Difficulty finding the confidence she needs to push herself beyond her comfort zone and I was hoping you could make her a weapon to give her that extra boost?"

She skipped on her toes, her short black hair flapping her silver eyes shining. "Oh yes! It would be my pleasure to assist you with that! What weapons are you comfortable with?" she asked me. I blew out a nervous breath and rubbed my hands together in front of me as I spoke, "Yeah, I um—have never used any weapon before. So I guess it's up to you."

She looked at me as if she were sizing me up and smiled. "Come here, let me get a feel for your life-force." I stepped closer, and she held my hands, closing her eyes for a few seconds and gasped. "I've got it!" *Thank God—because I sure don't.* Her hands were open out in front of her, she ran one over the other until a silver liquid and white light forming began swirling, forming a long, thin sword with a solid Jade handle. The blade looked sharp enough to cut you by staring at it. *This can't be for me.*

"I—I don't think I'm ready for that, I could kill someone with that thing!" She nodded, holding it out, encouraging me to take it. "That's the whole point silly! This, is a Katana; a lethal weapon—and it's your new best friend on the battlefield, you will slay many demons with it—trust me, take it. I'm never wrong when I choose a weapon, your life-force spoke to me, and this is what you *need.*" She pushed the Katana into my hands and closed my fingers around the base.

I felt a connection to the blade as it sang with my life-force, my Jade and Amber energy radiated off of it. "Whoa!" I stepped back giving myself space and sliced through the air in two angled chops. The blade was so fine, I could hear the air being cut leaving a high pitched chime as the metal charged through.

Eliza and Gideon cheered at my show. "You see?" Gideon began, "I knew you had a warrior's spirit, sometimes you need a little boost to bring it out!" The sword made me feel more powerful and helped me tap into my inner fighting instinct. *This is incredible.* It was more than just my confidence it boosted, I felt like I *could fight* for the first time in my life.

I looked at Gideon as I twirled the sword in my hands with ease, dancing my fingers around the handle. His eyes widened in awe, he dropped his jaw into a broad smile, "Whoa now, where d'you learn to do that love? "

"Well, I used to take baton." I stated, encasing my sword.

He shook his head, "You're telling me you can do *this* because you took baton?" and looked at Eliza. "Can you believe it?" Gideon was beaming with pride. "One more thing Jacey... to complete your arsenal." I stopped showing off and put my Katana away. "What else could I need?" She grinned and raised her eyebrows at me holding out her hands, I watched fascinated again by her creation as she held a smaller blade. “This is a Tanto, it goes with your Katana, carry it on your hip or lower leg where it will be accessible during battle.”

The Tanto had the same crisp blade as my Katana but smaller. Its handle was the same Jade material except for this one had a large emerald attached to its handle. I picked up the blade and admired it. “Wow” I whispered, jumping up to hug Eliza. “Thank you—thank you so much!” Like a true warrior, I attached the Tanto to my side and strapped the Katana on my back feeling a confidence I'd never had before and looked at Gideon. “I'm ready.”

Eliza came up and hugged me hopping up and down. “I'm so excited for you! Have fun and push your limits, it's the only way you'll get stronger—speaking of which, I should get back to *my* training.” I had been so caught up in my new weapons I didn't even notice the Arsenal and Elemental Angels battling all around us.

I watched them now and didn't feel the intimidation looming over me like I used to but rather, I felt excitement and couldn't wait to become even better with my blades Lucifer and Damien could bring their army of death to my door and death would answer their call, I'd make sure of that.

Gideon nudged me, "Well, let's get back to your training shall we, give you a chance to play with your shiny new toys?"

I raised my eyebrows, “Be careful what you wish for—I think I may take you now!”

“Well, you know the old saying, talk is cheap, Love.”

"Yeah, yeah, yeah. I'll show you talk is cheap." I said, shoving him into the sky laughing.

I stared up with overwhelming love at Gideon, he was my happy ending and I didn't know where I would be if it weren't for him. He could make any situation better, no problem was insurmountable to him and he gave me hope for the bright future ahead.

"Hey, you know what?" I asked.

"What's that Love?"

"I love you." His eyes gleamed, and he dipped into me. "Well, I love you too beautiful." A mischievous smile spread across his face, "but I hope you're not trying to butter me up to take it easy on ya, cause we're still going hard when we get back." I shook my head laughing, "Oh, I wouldn't dream of it being any other way."

CHAPTER TWENTY-EIGHT: KILL OR BE KILLED

We hovered for a moment looking at the field together. "What are we waiting for?" Gideon was quiet, still looking at the groups below. "I'm looking for Jesus, I thought we should show him what Eliza gave you, and how your skills have grown."

He continued to scan over the crowd and closed his eyes, searching for Jesus' thoughts I presumed, but he shook his head. "He's not here anymore. Oh well, we'll show him later. C'mon, let's go back to the Warriors, I want you to get as much practice with your weapons as possible." We flew to the other end of the field, dropping ourselves back into the group.

The Warriors were facing off with the Watchers, I had to find Maleki and show him my skills. I looked through both groups but I couldn't find him either. *Strange.... Where could they be?* "Don't worry about that, get your head in the game, it's time to train now." Gideon ordered. I turned around and faced him, shocked.

I couldn't believe he barked at me like that. "Excuse me? You can't talk like that!" He smiled "Are ya mad love? Good! Stop talking and fight me!" *Oh…. I see what he's doing.* "Fine. But just remember you asked for it!" As I pulled my Katana out from behind my back I hesitated, I didn't want to hurt Gideon even if he couldn't feel it or die from it. "Come on Jacey! We've been over this a thousand times, you're not going to hurt me. Besides, you probably won't even get the chance to, I'm faster than you—remember?"

"I don't care, I'm not taking any chances." His face shown frustration. "Do you not understand what we are trying to accomplish with this training? When the time for battle comes, it's either *kill---or be killed* I don't think I have to remind you they want us *dead* and you have little time to become a skilled fighter, you must if we hope to defeat them!" I sighed, Gideon was right I thought about his words and got hit with an idea.

That doesn't mean I have to chop my boyfriend into a million pieces. So I ran my hand over the blade and materialized a thin guard across the length. *There.* With my blade covered, I took my fighting stance holding it out in front of me and nodded to Gideon who just sighed, "You're so stubborn."

"But smart!" I held my sword with one hand motioning him to come at me with the other and we began our fight. I lunged forward with the blade, Gideon stepped aside and took me from behind, his arm wrapped around my throat, I thrust my elbow into his gut and he let out a grunt as his grip loosened. I dropped out of his hold turning around to face him and swung one leg under his feet. He jumped, avoiding the trip with ease. I stood up blocking his fist with the blade and kicked him hard, throwing him back.

We moved as if our fight was a dance back and forth we went blocking, hitting, and evading one another's attacks. As our dance continued, my speed increased, I could react and defend without thinking and he coached me perfectly, I was really beginning to get the swing of things. He was an excellent trainer and fighter and it was no wonder he led the Warrior Angels.

"From what we know, there are three types of beings we will face in Lucifer's army. The Fallen, The Dark Ones, and Lucifer's Beasts." I lunged forward again, missing Gideon by just a hair this time still fighting as I spoke. "Well—how do we kill them? Is there a certain way or…?" Gideon jumped back again, but the tip of my blade contacted his torso this time slicing across it.

I thanked God I had the foresight to put my guard over it before because I would have opened his stomach without it. "Aha! You see? I got you! I knew it was a good idea to put this on!" He chuckled and rubbed his stomach. "Yeah... but you wouldn't have hurt me... and that's not a kill shot either!" He thrust his hand down and materialized his own sword.

It was wider than my Katana and looked much heavier but he twirled it with ease and took a shot at me. I swerved my body and gave him a smug look as he missed. When he came at me again, I used my sword to block his attack. As we moved faster, the sound of our blades connecting chimed over and over creating a rhythmic hum in the air.

"What's a kill shot then?" I grunted out in between our movements.

Gideon jumped in the air flipping over my head, landing behind me and I froze as I felt the cold steel of his blade against my neck. "*This is a kill shot"* He lifted the blade away from my neck and I breathed a sigh of relief. "Okay—So we behead them?" *Gross.*

"Well, yes, severing the head from the body is the first step, the true kill comes from releasing their life-force from their chest." I thought back to when Lucifer tried to steal God's life-force remembering that it did come from the chest where your heart would be.

"I thought they didn't have life-force? How do we do that?" I could see by his expression I would not like the answer.

"Well, they have Lucifer's life-force, similar to the way we have Father's. You need to open the chest, The life-force will come out on its own... well, it's supposed to—I've never done it before but this is what Jesus has told us, and his information comes from The Watchers and Father." I nodded. "Okay, so now I have hand to hand combat down, let's work on kill shots." We faced off again. This time, I would go for the kill shots and make sure I succeeded.

"Good! That's great technique!" Gideon encouraged my every effort. As the training wore on I utilized my wings flapping to evade incoming attacks. I had all the gifts necessary to fight and win, and I was learning how to use them all in combat to my advantage.

"Can we take a break?" I breathed. Gideon nodded, and we stepped aside for a few minutes. "Where's Jesus and Maleki, they're still not back yet?" I was worried about them. He shrugged his shoulders. "I don't know, no one said anything I was so busy with our training I didn't even notice them leave."

Zahara and Eliza flew in and joined us with excitement all over their faces. "Have either of you seen Jesus or Maleki?" Gideon asked, they looked at each other and shrugged. "No, we haven't seen them since this morning when training began. Why?" Gideon looked onto the field and then at me, "It's nothing. I'm sure they'll be back soon enough."

The sky was growing darker, the sun, almost gone behind the horizon. The moons may have been large but they only let off a soft glow but not enough to see anything in. "Hey—how are we supposed to train in the dark?" It didn't seem safe to be sword fighting and arrow throwing in the middle of the night but what Jesus said was clear: we were to train round the clock until I mastered every aspect of battle.

Eliza dismissed my worry with her hand, "Oh, Ashira and the Elementals will whip us up fire orbs in the sky, it will be the same as daytime!" *Is there anything we can't do?* I shook my head, every time I had worried, I discovered more proof of how amazing we were.

Each Angel entrusted with a unique and powerful gift, my faith in our army had grown were strong, an unstoppable powerful force who could not only face Lucifer and his army, we could *defeat them.*

CHAPTER TWENTY-NINE: A RISK WORTH TAKING

Zahara and Eliza exchanged an anticipatory look. “Big news guys, I had an idea for a new weapon, so I asked Eliza if it would be possible and she thinks her and the Arsenals can create it!” Seeing as I had just witnessed the Arsenals gift firsthand, I was excited for Zahara and confident in Eliza. “That's great!” I said, giving them both a high-five. “What kind of weapon are we talking about here?” Gideon inquired.

Eliza leaned in to speak, “Well, it will be a wearable life-force device that can absorb the energy and channel a powerful beam.” she bit her lip in excitement. “Concentrating life-force in that manner will tear through large numbers of Lucifer's army—*this weapon* could turn the tides of war in our favor despite us being outnumbered.” She had a hopeful look in her eyes.

Gideon shook his head, he didn't look impressed either, he looked worried. “How would we be able to power such a weapon without depleting too much of our own life-force? We don't know how our bodies would react having it taken in large quantities and what you're proposing would require—*a lot*. Something like that could really hurt us."

He looked between them, "I'm sorry girls, but we cannot afford to waste our time creating and testing it—not with the situation we are in." His face turned serious, "The war *is imminent!* We *must* stick with what we *know and waste no time* if we hope to survive." We stood in awkward silence as Gideon's less than happy response to the proposed weapon was not what they expected.

Eliza's aggravation shown on her face, and she spoke matter-of-factly, "That is the whole point of a new weapon: to *give us more than a hope.* This could guarantee our victory! How can you not see this is a risk worth taking?" She looked at me. "Jacey has already shown great progress as a fighter and can *still* train with you while Zahara and I work out the logistics of the life-force gun. When it is complete Zahara and Jacey can practice operating the prototype since Healers have more--"

Gideon yelled cutting her off, "You're not using Jacey to power anything! She's not getting anywhere near it I forbid it so you can forget it!" hearing him speak for me made me outraged, I didn't even *want* to use the weapon but I would let no one speak for me as if I had no say in the matter. "Um—Excuse me? You do not make my decisions for me!"

"Jacey I--" I threw my hand up, "I don't want to hear it! Last I checked, I was a grown woman that could decide for herself thank you very much." I looked at the girls, "Let me know when you have a prototype ready I *want to help.*" I looked at Gideon like a rebellious child, he looked angry, pressing his lips in a thin line as if he might explode. "*Fine. Do whatever you want.*" He said through his teeth and dove into the sky, disappearing into the night.

That was the first fight we had ever gotten into, sadness and regret instantly filled me creating knots in my stomach. I stared up into the sky at the spot Gideon disappeared into for a long moment until Eliza spoke. "Oh don't worry about him! He's just mad you didn't go for his 'macho man' mode—great job you stood your ground and shut him down!" She made her hand dive towards the ground and they both laughed, but I couldn't find the humor in it.

I felt guilty that I had overreacted, I didn't even *want* to use a new weapon and only agreed to it out of spite—and that wasn't right either. *Damn.* Now Gideon was off somewhere with hurt feelings and mad at me and I had no idea where he would go.

I looked at the girls worried. "Do you guys know where Gideon lives?" Eliza snorted, "Are you serious? Jacey—let him cool off. He'll come back when he's done being mad. We need to focus on our new weapon!"

"That will wait." Maleki said as he and Jesus descended next to us and I saw the solemn look on their faces. "What's wrong?" I asked. Jesus stepped closer "Our father wishes to see you." Time stood still, it seemed as if everything around me froze in that moment I raised my hand and touched my face, shocked and whispered, *"God wants to see me?"*

CHAPTER THIRTY: TWO-WAY STREET

I took a moment to process what they'd just said and come out of my daze. *What would God want to see me for?* Maleki spoke, his urgency pulling me back to reality, "We *must go—now."*

Jesus grabbed my arm, "This is a great honor that many of the others have never had. *Our Father* wishes to see *you."* Gideon would have to wait. I shook my head clearing away my thoughts for the moment. "Yes—you're right." I uttered, I was shaking inside and my knees felt like they would fail me if I took a step.

"I can't believe this is happening--" I blew out a nervous breath trying to settle my stomach and rubbed my hands along my thighs. Jesus chuckled and thumped my back, "Relax—you need not be nervous or afraid and if it's any consolation, Maleki and I will be with you every step of the way." That helped, I wasn't afraid, but I didn't know what to expect and felt a guide to the formalities would be helpful. Eliza stepped forward with her finger raised, “Um—Jesus, Zahara and I have an idea for a new weapon we feel would--”

“I’m sorry Eliza, but it will have to wait until we return.” She nodded and Jesus sighed observing her disappointment. “I’m sure, whatever it is you two are working on is great and I can't wait to hear all about it first thing when I get back, okay?” Her face brightened as she flashed a smile. Jesus held his hands in front of him, moving them in a large circular motion and created a portal and looked at me, “Let’s go.” We stepped into the portal.

This portal differed from others I had been through; the tunnel seemed composed of glass, clear with flecks of color throughout the walls. A thick cloud-like mist covered the floor with rainbow swirls that came up over my calves causing the familiar tingle of portal travel. But the most outstanding part of this portal was *where* it was, because it seemed as if we were in outer space surrounded by billions of stars of all shapes, colors, and sizes. At the end of the portal was a giant galaxy radiating off of a center that burned with a bright white fire.

"It's incredible." I whispered as I moved forward. "Yes," Maleki began, "This is the Ascension portal for the Guardians, it is only accessible to Jesus, Father, and The ascending Guardians." I looked at him perplexed and he chuckled. "*We* are accompanying Jesus—we wouldn’t even be able to open it alone." I nodded "I see—so why does God want to see *me?"*

“Well, we're about to find that out.” Jesus answered, motioning with his hand, helping me through the exit of the portal.

We stood in a grand white room with thousands of globes covering the ceiling and walls. There was a giant platform and in its center stood six large beings. *The Guardians.*

They were enormous and wore long white hooded cloaks but they were without a body, I stared at them in a dumbfounded shock. The only thing visible beyond their cloaks was their life force—which was huge and let off a radiant glow. It reminded me of a circulatory system; the life-force was the heart yet it had dozens of strands branching off into what would be a body—if one were there.

I scanned the room gasping at the sight of him and tears fell. He was laying on a chaise lounge and looked sick. I walked towards him, he smiled and raised his hand reaching out to me. "Father," Jesus said rushing over to help him sit up. "This is Jacey." I was still crying, none of this seemed real and God looked like he was on his death bed.

He reached out to me and wiped my tears, resting his hand on the side of my face. "Do not weep my child, let your heart be joyous, for you are the key to victory in this war." I looked at him confused. *How?* He stood up, Jesus and Maleki held both of his hands helping him walk to the center of the room where the Guardians stood. Watching God take so much effort to walk just broke my heart, and I almost started another round of crying. He was so strong and vibrant when I saw him in my vision from the Well, strong enough to face Lucifer and win. *What happened?*

Jesus turned and motioned his head for me to come closer by their side and God spoke. “You're related by blood to Damien, son of Lucifer?” I shivered hard. The *last* thing I wanted to do was admit that I had a bloodline close to Lucifer, but it was true, so I nodded, wondering where this discussion was going.

“You've experienced Lucifer accessing your mind, even pulling you to his level of existence in person?” I nodded again, ashamed. God grinned, “That's good.” His turquoise eyes shined. “It's a two-way street you know—this *connection* between Damien and yourself.”

A two-way street? “What does that mean how does that help us?” God smiled again and raised his eyebrows raising a shaky finger. “Ah—*We* will pay our Damien a little visit ourselves—through you.” Just then his knees buckled, and he collapsed, Maleki and Jesus caught him in the nick of time, carrying him back over to the chaise lounge and laid him down.

I rushed over to his side and fell to my knees, “What's wrong with him?” I looked up to Jesus with pleading eyes. “Can I heal him?” I placed my hands over his chest but he reached up holding them between his soft frail hands and shook his head at me. “I'm afraid there's nothing you can do my dear girl. We must defeat Lucifer—to stop him from stealing my Children of Light and bring the universe back to its balance.” He closed his eyes and a single tear fell down his cheek.

"How can he have gotten so bad off?" I asked crying onto God's hands. Jesus and Maleki stood, solemn expressions on their faces, they shared the same heartache to see God this way. "He has given all of his life-force away." Jesus whispered, "Take a cup of water out of a fountain and dump it back in, you would never notice it left. But take a cup of water from a fountain and give it away, over and over, and the fountain runs dry."

He looked at me. “That has happened to our father, he has breathed life into millions of Children of Light intending for them to fulfill their destiny on earth and return home someday. But Lucifer has been corrupting them, stealing them and gaining massive amounts of strength while weakening our Father.”

Maleki reached down and helped me to my feet. “We will channel your life-force with the Guardians to create a force strong enough to hitchhike a ride into your brother’s mind using your connection. This takes an enormous amount of life-force, so expect to feel weak afterwards.” I would do anything to help God and if it gave us a leg up for the war, well that was all the more reason for me to do this. “Whatever it takes to bring him *down.”* I said.

Jesus guided me to the center of the group of Guardians and I stepped onto the circular pedestal, I noticed a north star shimmering at its center. The six guardians surrounded me, their cloaks floating around their bodiless life-force. Maleki strode up beside me and placed both hands on my temples, shocking me as we linked up. The swirls in his galactic eyes froze for a second, then swirled quickly as if there were a hurricane of stars in them. “Guardians, link up.” Jesus ordered.

The life-force of each Guardian reached out to the one next to it, linking to form a complete circle, a surge of power rushed through me as beams of light streamed from the Guardians. Maleki got a hit with the same powerful jolt I was and his eyes grew larger. “Concentrate on Damien, focus Jacey.” He yelled over the loud hum of the energy that surrounded us. I closed my eyes and pictured my brothers face chanting his name: *Damien. Damien. Damien.*

A dark tunnel appeared in my mind, Maleki was standing next to me and pressed his finger against his lips. We walked together through the dark passageway noticing a series of red doors as we tip-toed along opening each one a crack to peak inside.

CHAPTER THIRTY-ONE: DEMENTED

Behind each red door appeared to be a memory of some sort. Just like when I drank from the Well, it played in flashes and moved in fast forward. I saw Damien being born—from my mother. The doctor shook his head as my mother cried the anguished sobs of heartbreak any woman would have to know their child was stillborn.

But the doctor wasn't a *real doctor.* He rushed the baby away and delivered my little brother into Lucifer's waiting arms. *He was a Demon.* A Demon who had to have been working for Lucifer the whole time, whose sole purpose was to break my mother's heart and steal her son—Lucifer's son. Rage burned through me at the sight, Maleki closed the door and we moved on.

We opened door after door, revealing all the pain and agony Lucifer had put Damien through to mold him into the perfect, most evil weapon he could. With each memory I could understand Damien more and find compassion for him in my heart. My brother was not born evil, no, he was made evil and a victim of circumstance. A helpless child that grew up under the vile reign of a demented individual obsessed with power and revenge.

The horrors that played out behind each door were unthinkable: countless hours of brainwashing and intense, ruthless training. Damien's memories were of nothing but pain, power, and evil. Any attempt on his part to go against his Father and show mercy or compassion led to severe punishment. They beat Damien and starved him; he was attacked by packs of beasts and Demons and left nearly dead frequently.

I shuddered as I closed the door on my brother cowering in a corner, bleeding from one of his punishments for refusing to kill one of the stolen Children of Light his Father had brought before him. It was hard to watch such a scene play out.

We continued down the hallway Maleki nudged me and pointed to his head, he wanted to communicate, but I had never succeeded at doing so. With a helpless look and a shrug of my shoulders I thought, '*I can't do it—I can't hear anyone no matter how hard I try.*'

He gave me an exasperated look, insisting that I try, so I closed my eyes and focused finding his voice. *'We need to be very careful now, we are heading into his consciousness—he might detect us here.'*

My face lit up. *'I hear you! What happens if he knows we're here?'*

Maleki looked at me. *'We won't be able to find what we're looking for and this will have been a gross waste of life-force—for everyone.'* I nodded, we had to move faster now.

At the end of the passageway was a larger door, Maleki grabbed the handle and twisted, but it wouldn't open. *'This must be it. His consciousness; It's locked away for a reason there must be a key to open it.'* He examined the door, looking for the key and I remembered God saying I was the 'key' to this plan working. On a hunch, I reached out for the handle.

'It's locked; it won't open.' I turned the handle and heard a soft 'click' as the lock released and opened the door only an inch. *'I don't believe it.'* Maleki said with a hint of wonder. We peaked through the narrow crack and listened. Damien and Lucifer were discussing their plan to overthrow Heaven.

"He's weak—we could take him now." Damien said, pounding his fists on the table.

"No, the time is not right--" Lucifer stood lacing his fingers in front of him. "We wait until their healer ascends—your sister will give them a false sense of security—then, when the eclipse comes and darkness rules the earth---we will be at our most powerful--"

Damien finished the thought, "Then we attack and destroy them all!" Lucifer cackled. "Then my dear boy—with Heaven gone and The Angels out of the way, we'll take your *sister* and be a family like you've always wanted."

I gasped and covered my mouth with my hand, they stiffened. "Someone's here." Lucifer said We shut the door and ran down the hallway out of Damien's mind for good I hoped. When we reached the end of the portal, I reconnected with my body and opened my eyes with a relieved sigh, I was back in God's chamber in the circle of Guardians. Maleki came back into his body and dropped his hands from my temples.

We were panting, my mind still felt a little foggy, I had never felt so weak and utter exhaustion overcame me. My knees buckled, and I fell to the floor. "Jacey!" Jesus scooped me up into his arms. "Bring another bed for her!" He ordered the Guardians. They broke apart, and another bed materialized next to where God was and he laid me down.

"I—I'm sorry." I mumbled. "Shh—you poor girl, stop apologizing and let your life-force recharge, you must relax." Maleki's face came into view and I smiled. *'Tell him what we found out.'* He nodded and smiled, "I will—you can rest Jacey." *'Okay,"* I closed my eyes, falling asleep.

CHAPTER THIRTY-TWO: REST AND RECUPERATION

I was still in God's chambers when I opened my eyes and felt better, but the exhaustion lingered. I looked over and saw God resting, his eyes were still closed. "I'm awake." He said, "Just resting, as should you." He opened his beautiful eyes and looked at me, smiling. "You did a very brave thing, you saved us all. You should be very proud of yourself young lady, I know I am."

He reached his feeble hand across the space between us and patted mine. "Oh, I wish I could talk with you more my dear but I must rest and conserve my life-force." I nodded and got up, walking around our beds and leaned over to hug my creator. "I love you God. We will fix this and restore the balance." He rubbed my back. "I love you too my child." He whispered.

He looked at Jesus and Maleki, then back at me, "You should go... join the others—don't worry about me, I have my Guardians here to help care for my needs." I nodded. It was a bittersweet moment, saying goodbye to God, and I wondered if I would ever see him again, and what would happen after we defeated Lucifer. *Would God get better? How does that even work?*

I walked over to Jesus and Maleki. "Jacey!! Well done! Because of you, we have the missing piece!" He wrapped me in his arms and swung me around squeezing me and laughing, he was in an ecstatic mood. His high spirits, a refreshing change from the radiating sense of impending doom that had lingered around us.

I smiled. "Yes, the night of the eclipse—but when is that?"

Maleki answered, "On earth time? About a month. For us? About a week."

My eyes widened, "That's—so soon."

Jesus wrapped his arm around me. "Yes, we have little time, but don't worry. Between your progress with Gideon in training, the new weapon, and us knowing when to expect them, there is not a doubt in my mind we *will* be victorious—together!"

I choked. *Gideon! Oh no!* I had all but forgotten about the fight we had before they summoned me. *I wonder if he's still mad at me. Does he know I had to leave? I have to get back. What if he's looking for me? But what about God?* I looked over my shoulder, he was laying so still it almost looked like he was dead. I gave Jesus a worried look, "He—he will get better after we defeat them, right?" He looked at me swaying his head.

"I wish it were that simple Jacey, I do. But, the only thing that will help Father is to restore the balance of good and evil. The first step is the victory in war but that's only half the battle; we still need to restore balance on *Earth."* He motioned to all the globes covering the walls of God's chambers. "Each of these spheres are a Child of Light… Come, I'll explain it to you."

We walked up to the closest wall, I could see inside each sphere was a unique color no bigger than a marble. There were blues, silvers, browns, jades, violets, and tiny milky way galaxies scattered. I noticed some of them were solid white, others laced with red and black.

"Why are they all different colors?" Jesus pointed to one that had Jade in it. "This is a future Healing Angel. This one will be a watcher, this one a Warrior, and so on and so forth. The ones like this--" He pointed to a red and black streaked sphere, "Are in danger of losing their right to ascend—Lucifer's demonic influencers have grown powerful enough to contaminate Children of Light at an alarming rate. Which is why the Guardians play such an important role in maintaining the balance, without them and with father's own life-force depleted, we are all in danger. Father has been bearing the brunt of the loss of life-force, but he can only take this for so long and we are running out of time. That is why it's so important for us to win this war."

Jesus walked over to his Father and knelt beside him, saying goodbye. A tear fell from my eye and slid down my cheek as he placed a hand on his son's face and Jesus wept into his palm. I felt the sting of more tears pricking at my eyes and my chin quivered.

"It will be okay Jacey." Maleki whispered from behind me. I had forgotten he was standing there and jumped as he leaned in closer, "*Trust me.*" I nodded, wiping the tears away from my face as Jesus stood up and walked back towards us.

His worry was all over his face but he forced a smile, "Let's get back shall we? I'm sure Zahara and Eliza will have made progress on their weapon. And you need to continue your training with Gideon." My heart sank into my stomach at the mention of his name. I didn't even know what I would say to him, but we had to make up it was the only thing on my mind as we went through the portal, back to Heaven.

When we slipped out the other side, it was daylight already and the training field was still wet from morning dew. Rays of sunlight peaked through the trees creating streams of pink, yellow, and orange—it was breathtaking and refreshing. The sky was full of the bright colors I had now grown so accustomed to; pinks, purples, turquoises, and shimmering white.

The field was alive with the clamour of clashing weapons and grunts as the Angels went at it with everything they had. "All right," Jesus made his normal thunderous noise with a clap of the hands and everyone stopped, "Angels, gather around, we have big news!"

They surrounded us, I scanned the crowd for Gideon's face. "Brothers, sisters," I moved through the crowd hoping to find

Gideon, Jesus' voice trailed off as I moved further into the crowd and he told the Angels about what Maleki and I accomplished. *Where is he?* Worry filled me, leaving a sick feeling in my gut.

Gideon was mad about Zahara's idea but I couldn't understand *why.* I mean, he was the one who was pushing me to train so hard—to fight with everything in me. He was the one who took me to Eliza and got me my Katana and Tanto blades. He didn't have a problem with my fighting—he encouraged it, so what was the big deal about the new weapon?

"Jacey!" I heard Zahara's familiar voice and pushed through to find her. She and Eliza were both standing at the back motioning for me to come over with wide grins. I peaked over my shoulder at Jesus who was still speaking to the other Angels planning for the next seven days as we awaited the attack. Eliza had a look of satisfaction and pride. "We have a prototype! The other Arsenals and I worked all night! Come on—you gotta see this thing!"

I hesitated. I had to find Gideon and set things right before I did anything else. Zahara looked at me and touched Eliza's shoulder, "Jacey has something she needs to do first." Her mouth opened, "Oh yes." she smirked at me. "You'll come find me when you've finished?" I nodded, "I won't be long! Tell Jesus I went to look for Gideon if he asks please?" They gave me a thumbs up as I leapt into the sky, I had an idea where Gideon was, and hoped I was right.

CHAPTER THIRTY-THREE: KISS AND MAKE-UP

The first order of business is to find out where Gideon lives after all of this. Then, I need to work on my navigation skills. I'm tired of never knowing where I am or how to get somewhere. Ugh! This is ludicrous! Why am I driving myself crazy over this? Look at me! Just look! I'm flying through Heaven, in the middle of a crisis so I can find the man I love and put an end to this ridiculous fight.

I flew alone with my thoughts scanning every area I passed over while I was on my way to where it all began: the ascension portal. *He has to be there… I hope. I mean, it makes sense—that's where I would go if I were him. But, I'm not him am I? No, because if I were him, I wouldn't get all huffy over an experimental weapon that could change everything for the better in this war! Please, please be there Gideon…*

I knew deep down I would find Gideon at the portal. It was where our journey had begun with one another, where his boyish charm, energy, wit, and attractiveness first worked its magic on me. This was the place where I felt the connection we shared—even if I denied it with every fiber of my intellect. It all started *here.* Although I didn't know where I was going, I trusted my instincts and focused all of my energy on feeling Gideon.

In the distance, I saw the evergreen mountains with the trademark falls cascading down both sides. I knew I was in the right place so I descended at the base of the mountain and climbed up the narrow floral filled trail. Seeing the familiar canopy of bright colors and listening to the birds sing with the roar of the waterfalls in the background brought upon me a sense of calm as I climbed.

The scenery was beautiful and as I trekked higher; I felt proud remembering how far I had come in such a short amount of time. I had gone from a normal shy, scared girl, to a Katana wielding Angel in God's army that could kick your ass—and Heal it afterwards, I smiled to myself at the thought.

Now, I donned the same clothes I once thought were so strange and felt like I belonged, this was my home. *And that is the man I love.* Gideon looked up at me and forced a smile. "Hey." he waved his hand. My brow furrowed. "'Hey'? That's all I get? Okay, that stings--" I came and sat down next to him. The silence was deafening.

I sighed, if anyone would fix our fight, I guess it had to be me. "Look, I— I don't *understand* why this was such a big deal to you, I mean, you don't care if I get stabbed, punched, cut, or kicked but flip out over Eliza and Zahara's idea of a powerful life-force weapon?" I shook my head.

Gideon had his lips pressed in a thin line and was bouncing his knee up and down. He looked at me and grabbed my hand pressing my fingers to his temple. My eyes went blank, and I saw an array of visions, he was allowing me inside his head, projecting his memories into my mind.

There was a beautiful woman with bright red hair and vivid blue eyes, she had fair skin kissed with freckles and dressed in old style clothing—perhaps from the early 1900s.

I saw the love in her eyes as she looked at me and tickled her nose against mine, laughing and running away through the green pastures. There was a cozy little shack with a flock of sheep and a few scattered chickens. I felt the love and peace that only comes from finding your happiness on Earth.

More blurs came and went of loving memories, ocean side picnics, family gatherings—men came to the door, they were soldiers with papers they were asking for me to enlist and help defend Ireland. I read the scroll, shook their hands and signed it---Gideon McGrath, 1919. The woman cried and begged me to stay, I left anyway. We trained, we fought, I was shot---there was too much blood, the doctors rushed to save me but it was already too late. I saw a bright face—a Guardian and went through the portal where Jesus awaited me.

Gideon removed my hand from his temple and broke the connection. I was crying. "Oh my God!" I sat there catching my breath after having lived Gideons last moments, I looked at him, pulling my hand from his and demanded, “Who was that woman?” Staring at him in a state of shocked panic. “Wh—Are you—you're *married*?” I shrieked.

He was quiet for a moment, looking down at his hands before he nodded. “Yes, I mean— I was, back in my human life... her name was Mary I loved her, I enlisted to protect her—to protect our future family together never thinking it would be the last time I’d see her again.” I shook my head in utter disbelief. “Well? Is she here?” my mind was dumbfounded as I tried to remember the memory. “1919--- that was like— 100 years ago!”

I stood up borderline hyperventilating, filled with mixed emotions. Sad for Gideon’s loss, angry he didn’t tell me about his wife, and confused because that didn’t explain why he had gotten so mad before. I threw my hands up in the air, frustrated. “Please say something to make this all—MAKE SENSE! Because all I can gather is that you kept your wife a secret from me and that's fine, but I want to help *our* friends—*our family*—defeat an army of Demons and save the world and somehow *I’m* the one who’s wrong and you're the one who's upset?!”

“No, No! You’re not in the wrong Love— you don’t understand, you were never in the wrong. I’m sorry if you felt that way.” He jumped to his feet, “When I ascended—I struggled with everything, the same as you did! I mean, to be a Warrior Angel, a leader but to find out my wife didn't share the same destiny as I. Eternity— well, it wasn't possible for us. She lived her life to fullest on Earth and ascended to Paradise Valley when the time came and she found love, remarried, and had children— I'm happy for the life she lived."

He was speaking so fast it was hard to keep up, "Jacey, I *never* thought I would find love again after I had been here 100 years alone. Sure, I had brothers, sisters for friends and my family of Angels---but *love* eluded me. Other Angels were pairing through the years; even Jesus paired with Zahara— and I longed for the other half of my pair--" Confused, I put my hand up to stop him, "Pairing? Wait—what did you say? Jesus and Zahara?" *Well, I guess they seem close*— wow, g*ood for them. That's freaking awesome.*

He came up and draped his hands around my shoulders, looking me in the eyes and kissed my forehead. "Your mind is all over the place Love, I can barely keep up with your thoughts! It's part of why I love you so much you know--" He ran his hand down my face, holding his palm against my cheek.

"Pairing---it's like the Heavenly matrimony. When Angels pair—it's for eternity with the other half to your whole—your soul mate, you only have one. Your life force *connects*—and it's a connection stronger than anything you can imagine. One I had all but given up on—*Until I met you*."

"When I saw you for the first time, I knew in my gut, in my *heart,* and soul you were my other half. My eternal half and from the moment you ascended, I knew you felt it too--" He pointed to my temple tapping and chuckled. *Well, yeah..* "The feeling we have when we touch--" He ran his fingers down my arms and laced his fingers between mine. The electric humming of my life-force pulsating; it flowed through me to Gideon and back again. In my spine, my skin, my gut, every inch of my body inside and out hummed.

"Do you get it now? You became my charge, and I watched you and protected you until it was your time to ascend and join us. *I loved you long before you ever knew.* I got upset because their 'idea'" he put his fingers up in little quotations, "--this life-force gun—whatever it is, it's a great *idea.* But everyone seems to forget that life-force is scarce. I feared if something went wrong and you lost all of yours, there would be no way for you to ascend and I'd lose you."

He dipped his head down maintaining my eye contact. "Do you know what that would mean?" He shook his head, "I *can't* let that happen, not after I finally found you! *I can't lose you, I love you too much."* He held both of my hands rubbing them with his thumbs and looked up at me. His big blue eyes peaked through his curly bangs, pleading with me. "Sorry Love, I'm sorry for everything, I should have told you about Mary, but it was another life and it never seemed like the right time for that conversation. Can you ever forgive me?"

I wrapped my arms around his neck and rested my head on his chest. "Yes! And, I shouldn't have gotten all worked up. 100 years is an awfully long time, so I guess it's not so bad. You lived a life before you ascended, I won't hold that against you." He lifted my chin with his index finger and kissed me with a fiery passion.

What a way to make up. We should fight more often. He was reading my thoughts and laughed through our kiss. “You're crazy, woman.” He growled and kissed me again, picking me up. Every part of me was alive, I could feel our life-force blending together in perfect harmony and wanted to hold on to this moment, just the two of us, in love and alone. No Damien, no Lucifer and no war. I ran my hands along his neck and my fingers up through his curly hair. He pulled me closer to him, squeezing my waist setting me back down on my wobbly legs.

I let out a ragged breath and fanned myself. “Whew! That was—*intense.”* Gideon raised his eyebrows giving me a flirtatious smirk, “Oh, you ain't seen nothing yet, Love.” I giggled, “Oh? So you're holding out on me eh?” He held my hand and kissed it running his soft lips along my skin, sending small shivers up my arm and down my spine. “Patience is a virtue--”

“Okay, fair enough… besides--” I tapped my finger to his chest and pushed him back with it, “*you,* ain't seen nothing yet *either!”* He grabbed my wrist and pulled me into his embrace, kissing the tip of my nose. “Oh yeah?” I nodded, “Yeah.” he bit his lip and looked to the sky, “Well I guess we'll both have to practice our patience then, huh?” I kissed his cheek and whispered in his ear, “I guess so.”

We held each other for a long time, it felt good to get back to comfortable silence with him. As the sun shone brighter, I remembered Jesus and all the others were already back to training and Gideon had missed everything. I looked at him, “We have got to get back! There's so much to tell you! We have great news! Come on!" I dove into the sky with Gideon tight on my heels as we headed back to the training field.

CHAPTER THIRTY-FOUR: PROMISE

As we flew back to the field, I filled Gideon in on my visit with God. "Jesus and Maleki came and got me and we all went to see God, he theorized that my connection with Damien was a two-way street and hoped we could combine the Guardians life-force with mine. Maleki hijacked my connection with Damien and we rode it all the way to his consciousness.

"When we got into Damien's head, we went down a long hall with a bunch of doors that held his memories, it was so weird--" I shook my head. "Weird how?" I squinted my eyes thinking about the travesties that had befallen my brother and how Lucifer was such a monster, I swallowed hard. "Well, for starters, we saw pretty much every significant event that had ever happened to him in his entire—existence. And it was bad, like *terrible.* Lucifer and one of his demons tricked my mother into thinking Damien was *dead at birth and* stole him from her—from us. As I watched every memory play out well... I kinda felt *bad for him*--"

Shaking my head again, I continued, "We got to the door that led to his most protected memory but Maleki tried to open it and he couldn't. But when *I* tried it, it opened right up, and we saw the plan. They are coming the night of the eclipse—something about 'darkness will rule the Earth' they'll be at their most powerful then. Anyway, it's a week from now, we have a date." I shifted my gaze to Gideon, he had a determined look set on his face. "We'll be ready and so will you, I'm sure of it."

He always knew what I needed to hear, a pro of the whole telepathic thing. I was glad that the attack would no longer be a 'surprise' but it didn't change how I felt nowhere near confident in my abilities or ready to take them into battle yet. I would fight *whether I was ready or not*. Gideon had taught me so much and helped me grow, I knew he would continue to train me and I could only get better over the next week.

But fear still lingered inside me. The fear of not being skilled enough or fast enough to fulfill my destiny; to save the other Angels and defend Paradise Valley by defeating Lucifer's army. It was the reason for my creation, my purpose and role in Heaven, but the possibility of me failing God, Jesus and the others shook me to the core, leaving a dark knot twisting away inside me.

I had already seen the horrors of what lay ahead for us when I drank from the Well but didn't know if I was ready to witness them firsthand, or if I would ever be. There were lives at stake, billions of lives in Heaven and on Earth would suffer at the merciless hands of Lucifer if we failed. I thought about what he had done to his own son, sick from the memory of Damien's torture. *Thinking about it changes nothing.*

The colorful plains and rolling hills exuded the life, peace, and happiness of God's promise to us. The promise that if we made it to this place, we would spend eternity in peace and beauty, I never would have thought the promise came at a price, yet here we were, preparing to fight for and pay it.

Damien kept weighing on my mind. "Do you wanna talk about it?" Gideon prodded. I didn't want to, but I needed to get it out; try to process my feelings. "It's Damien I—can't help but think he *wanted* us to know when they are coming. You know? Like, maybe he wanted to help us, to *help me.* I know, it's absurd but some part of me feels like--- he's not *evil.* Why would his most important memory open right up for me in his mind?"

Gideon scoffed, "Are you serious? It's some genetic glitch, you and Damien share similar life-force because of your mother. He may not have even known you and Maleki were in his mind! Look, I know that you feel bad for him, he's your brother and I know it can change the way you view him. Just don't let it cloud your judgement Love, Damien *is the son of Lucifer, born* and raised with one purpose: to destroy Heaven and God.

"Even *if* and it's a small 'if' he *wanted* to help, there will always be an ulterior motive. He's evil Love, I'm sorry but there's nothing that can ever change that." I looked away. "You didn't see what I saw. *He didn't want to hurt anyone. That monster forced him to against his will."* He reached down, grabbing my hand, giving it a reassuring squeeze. "Well, that's true, I didn't. But none of that matters much, anyway. The fact is, we are about to fight an army of demons—and Damien is leading it. Nothing you saw in his past, can change that."

He was right. We were seven days away from the biggest war that has ever been and my brother was on the wrong side. *Will I have to fight him? Can I do what is necessary if it comes down to it?* Gideon was listening, "You won't be in that situation Love, I'll make sure. Okay? Right now we need to focus on your training." He motioned towards the field as it came into view and dipped his head towards me. "Head in the game princess. Your training is about to get—*intense."*

CHAPTER THIRTY-FIVE: BEST INTEREST

We headed into the field and stopped in our tracks, hovering in the air above the outer treeline, as Angels gathered around watching Eliza and Zahara strap on the life-force gun prototypes. It differed from anything I would have imagined; made of metal and had the color platinum. Yet despite being metal, it seemed pliable and moved molding with around your shoulders, resting on your chest.

Excitement rushed through me as I watched them focus their life-force. The weapon itself was one with their bodies as if it were alive and light streaked orbs ran down the straps forming a bright ball of concentrated energy in the center of the chest.

"Stand back!" Jesus yelled as everyone cleared a larger space. Eliza fired first, the bright beam was a bluish white and cut straight ahead, carving a perfect hole through a dozen large oaks. The crowd screamed and celebrated the success of the new weapon.

It was Zahara's turn to fire and held on longer than Eliza, charging up her weapon more. The unit glowed and trembled, shaking her entire body with the excess energy it was holding. She fired and flew back from the recoil as the beam released from her chest with an explosion, slicing through a half acre of the tree line, taking the tops clean off.

She could not gain control of the beam; it whipped her body around and came towards us. I froze in fear. *Oh my God.* "Jacey!" Gideon wasted no time, diving on me in a panic, sending both of us spiraling to the ground. We hit with the velocity of a mack truck behind us.

The impact from our bodies was so hard, it left a massive hole in the field. I felt crushed under Gideon's weight until he peeled himself off of me and scrambled to his feet. "Are you all right Love?" he asked. "Yeah—I'm fine." I coughed. Zahara dropped down into the hole crying, "I'm so sorry!" she cried out.

Gideon helped me up to my feet, we had cuts and bruises and I felt a few broken ribs moving when I poked my side. "Here, let me heal you both. I'm so sorry!" She sat us down, tears streaming on her face as her glowing hands ran up and down our bodies. With our wounds gone Zahara relaxed, letting out a huge relieved sigh.

"Whew!" she laughed. "That was a close one! Didn't see you guys there boy I didn't expect it would have such a kick!" I chuckled. Gideon glared at Zahara. "I said I was sorry." She mumbled. He clenched his jaw and nodded. Jesus jumped down into the crater sized hole we were sitting in and helped Zahara to her feet hugging her and kissed her forehead.

"I'm so glad you're all right." He said caressing her head as she rested it on his chest. "Did you see how powerful it was? It worked! I knew it would!" Jesus beamed in approval. For the first time, I could *see* the difference in the way he held Zahara's gaze. His eyes were softer when theirs met, his face relaxed. I wondered how I could have missed that.

"You did well! I will have Eliza and the Arsenals fit every Angel for their life-force gun, we need to train with them." Gideon broke his silence, "Have you gone mad?! She almost killed Jacey with that thing just now! It's obvious we can't control it! How could you even think this is a good idea?" He roared.

Jesus' face grew impatient, and he just snapped. "The last time I checked *I* was the leader of this army who are you to be questioning my decisions now?" He paused and took a breath to collect himself. "You must stop putting your feelings for Jacey in front of the best interest of everyone else, there is too much at stake here!"

Gideon held his ground. All Zahara and I could do was stand back and watch as the men we loved bickered, each driven by their own sense of what was right, each biased in their own way, because of their love for us. We glanced at each other with matching helpless expressions.

"You know well and good that the *only* reason, you even considered a life-force powered weapon as an option for this group was because it was Zahara's idea! Don't come at me as if I am the only one guilty of putting his feelings first! Come on Jesus, a life-force powered weapon when we are running out of life-force?! You would have never even *considered* it had Eliza approached you with it and not Zahara!"

Jesus looked indignant, "Do not think because you are my friend you are above reproach Gideon! How *dare you* presume to know what I would and would not do! Who are you anymore? I allowed this weapon because I believe it is our *best chance* at defeating Damien and Lucifer with the least amount of casualties from combat. Is it risky? Yes. But so is hand to hand combat where we are at an even bigger risk of coming in contact with their venom!"

Gideon interjected, "That's what they're here for!" motioning towards Zahara and I. "There's only two of them Gideon and thousands of us and hundreds of thousands in Lucifer's army! Do the math and be realistic, please! They could *never* get to everyone in time! Hundreds would perish, can't you see that these new weapons give *all of us* a better chance at surviving, at winning? Or are you so blinded by love that Jacey is now the only one for whom you care about?"

That did it, Gideon's eyes flashed with sadness as Jesus' words sunk in. He stood in his chagrin. I wanted to know what he was thinking and focused on Gideon. His voice came into my mind, I was in his thoughts.

'He's right. I've only been thinking about Jacey… When did I stop caring about the others safety and the greater good?' His face grew softer, his eyes, apologetic. "You're right, Jacey's safety has been the only thing that matters. I'm sorry Zahara, I think your weapon can help us win this war."

Excitement flashed in his eyes, "Let's get our new weapons." And opened his arms wide for a hug "Can you guys forgive me for being a total arse? I'm sorry for questioning you sir." He muffled to Jesus from the center of our embrace and we laughed.

"No worries my friend, I'm glad you found your pair, it's all the more reason for us to do whatever is necessary to defeat Lucifer. So we may all live in the promise of Father, restore the balance and enjoy the fruit of that promise, that is all I want for us." Jesus said.

"Are you guys staying in that hole all day or what?" Eliza's small voice called down to us. "We need to fit everyone for their life-force guns…" We had gained an audience; all the Angels surrounded the hole watching the argument play out. I smirked at Gideon and yelled, "Us first!" as we flew out.

CHAPTER THIRTY-SIX: HOME FIELD ADVANTAGE

“Hold still, this will tingle.” Eliza stated as she formed the liquid silver onto my body, creating the mold that would give life my personalized weapon. “It only works for you.” she continued, “We tune Each life-force gun to its Angel's unique frequency, only you can charge it so make sure you don't get it mixed up with anyone else's.” I pulled at the bands adjusting it as it took shape on me.

"It feels kind of tight." She pulled my hands down with a scolding look a mother would give. "It’s *supposed* to be. You need a good snug fit so it can bond with your life-force with the least amount of kick back—do you prefer your chest caved in, or a tight somewhat uncomfortable fit?" My eyes widened, "Um, I'll stick with the latter." I said, wriggling my shoulders.

Gideon was to my right getting fitted and looked like he was dealing with the same issues of the constraining life-force gun.

The Arsenals had their work cut out for them; there were still thousands of Angels in need of a fitting waiting in neat lines along the training field.

I felt the tingling cease and looked down at the finished product, it looked more advanced high-tech and futuristic than I would have thought. I could see the inner workings of the bands that wrapped around my shoulders all the tubes fed into the circle was on my chest.

They would act as the conductors for my life-force and funnel it into the center where it would concentrate and create the beam I had saw from the test run. “All done!” Eliza chirped with a slap on my arm. “You can go to Zahara and Jesus now, they'll get your training started.”

"Great! This is—it's amazing, you guys should be proud. I could have never thought of something like this let alone imagine how it could work." Her short dark hair bounced as she did a little bow. "Thank you, new challenges keep us sharp and creative!" She gave me a quick hug and kissed me on the cheek ushering me away, "Now, go practice!"

Zahara noticed me as I approached her and Jesus and flashed a satisfied smile. “Oh well, well, well. Look at your girl right here! You do *not* look like the same person I met at dinner that night.” Her Jade eyes sparkled, the contrast from her tan skin and dark hair made them stand out. I grinned at my beautiful sister and did a little twirl. “Thank you! I feel like I've grown so much since I ascended. So, what do you say? Want to show me how to use this thing?" Hooking my fingers beneath the straps I rocked back on my heels.

She clasped her hands together in front of her rubbing them, "Okay, so, the weapon works by a charge given off by your own life-force." I nodded, "You need to focus your energy, the same way you would if you were creating something—or healing. Try to think of it as a part of you, like you were bending your knees about to make a huge leap or something—you focus, then release." She took a step back, "Just don't hold it for too long, or you'll end up making the same mistake I did. We'll save those power shots for *actual* war."

"Okay, I think I got it. Simple enough." I took a wide stance and held my breath. "Nice and easy…." Finding my life-force frequency was easy. It was such a huge part of being here I could feel it humming through me like a heartbeat, at all times. So I focused on the humming, tuning it in. I saw the weapon light up, activated by the surge of my energy and smiled to myself. *I did it!*

When I could see the energy flowing through the bands, resting at the center, I released it with ease. The small beam shot out ahead of me, burning a perfect hole through the center of the trees. I watched as several trees fell over and shrieked jumping up and down with Zahara like a child.

"I did it! Did you see that? Can you believe it?!"

"Yes! I can believe it! I knew you would get the hang of it right away!"

"Whoa! Nice shot there, Love." I whirled around, Gideon was there admiring my handiwork, his life-force gun settled on him now and more Angels were coming up to join us with theirs. Jesus walked into the center of the now growing group to establish order in training. "Line up here." He motioned his arm in a straight line parallel with the trees, I stepped back out of the way.

"We need everyone to be an expert marksman with your life-force guns. You cannot afford to waste your shots in battle." He paced along the line like the true commander he was. "With that said, this is a simple exercise: you will learn to power up your weapon and fire it. No more, no less." He motioned to his mate, "Zahara, if you would please."

I watched Gideon stand in line with the other Angels as Zahara walked them through the same way she did for me. Gideon looked *good* with his life-force gun fitted around his muscular chest. *Perfection. He is pure perfection in every sense.*

He smiled, giving me a bashful glance. I covered my face with my hand to hide my guilty smile. The weapons cut the entire tree line down like a laser leaving nothing behind but burning stumps. "Whoa!" Gideon exclaimed along with the other Angels. "Did you see that?" He came over with the energy a boy with a brand new toy would have

"It's the most powerful weapon we could ever have." Jesus answered as he approached with Zahara.

For the first time, I realized Maleki was nowhere around, this concerned me. "Where's Maleki? I haven't seen him since we got back." Gideon looked around the field.

"Taking the Watchers to scan every possible entrance into Heaven that Damien can take." Jesus answered, "We know *when* the attack will be, but we still need to know *where.* We have the home field advantage in this war but it's most pressing we keep Heaven's damage to a minimum. If we don't know what entrance they'll use, the damage could be astronomical—and if they breach the force field around Paradise Valley—it would be deadly to its inhabitants."

A sharp pang hit my chest with the realization that the countless innocents had no way to defend themselves. "So where do you *think* the attack could take place?" I asked Jesus, concerned.

"With Fathers condition deteriorating, the barrier around Heaven grows weaker by the day." He shook his head, looking at us. "It could happen *anywhere* at this point but my guess is the ascension portal; where all newcomers come. He could access it by hitching to an ascending soul from Earth and with his demons crawling over every inch—it's possible for them to tear through the portal to create their opening." He ran his hands over his head, exhaustion from the stress clear on his face.

Gideon spoke, "The ascension portal doesn't give us a great angle for attack seeing as it's on a mountain—that would be a smart move on their part to put us in a bad defensive position." and paced in thought.

Something clicked inside me; a possibility they hadn't mentioned. "What about the Garden of Eden? Where the Well of Knowledge is now, it's where God cast Lucifer out and would seem like poetic justice to use the same portal they exiled him from for his army to come back and destroy us."

Jesus pondered my words. "He has never fallen short with his theatrics in the past. The irony of it— sounds like something Lucifer would do." He looked at Gideon, "Let's go find Maleki and The Watchers, examine the Well for any weakness in the barrier and set up a defensive strategy."

Gideon approached me to say goodbye Cradling my face between his large hands, he rested his forehead against mine. It had all happened so fast. *Us.* We'd barely gotten to spend any real amount of time together. It seemed like there was always *something.* Something we needed to do, or plan for, or figure out, besides us. None of it mattered though, I loved him, he was mine I was his to him, together, we were the perfect pair.

I brushed the wild blonde curls out off of his face resting my hand on his stubbled cheek. Life-force hummed a symphony between us that only we could feel. My eyes locked with his, the vibrant blue swirls hypnotizing me as they'd always done, "Keep training Love, I'll be back before you know it."

He pressed his lips against my head, I closed my eyes. "Be careful, I love you." The breeze from his wings blew my hair, he was gone when I opened my eyes. Zahara came up beside me and wrapped her arm around my shoulders. "We got ourselves good ones don't we?" she smiled. "Yeah, we sure do."

She sighed, the satisfied sigh that only true love could produce from a woman. "C'mon. Let's get this training done with the new life-force guns, want to help me?" I looked at the broken, abused trees and laughed. "I don't think these poor things can take any more practice."

"Pfft… they'll be fine." She said with a dismissing wave of the hand.

CHAPTER THIRTY-SEVEN: SISTER

We worked tirelessly, training each group of Angels to use their new weapons as they were fit with them. As night fell, The Elementals placed hundreds of fire orbs into the sky leaving the golden glow of a campfire on everything below. When the final group had finished their round, all that remained of the trees surrounding our field was burning embers.

Bewildered, I stared at the amount of destruction our weapons had done with the Angels firing only once and knew in my heart that they were going to be the key to our victory. Zahara sat down, leaned back with her arms supporting her as she looked up into the fiery night sky. Her thick braid was so long it rested on the ground behind her. "Come, take a quick break, we earned it." she patted the ground beside her.

I should be training. There's not much time left… "I don't know---" I hesitated, conflicted with the temptation of rest. "Jacey—sit with me for two minutes. Trust me, we will train plenty, I want us to enjoy a small moment together." Her smile was irresistible, I plopped down beside her and felt my muscles relax.

Being mentally and emotionally exhausted was taking its toll, the cool ground felt good underneath me. I layed back with my hands beneath my head with my eyes closed.

“There, you see? What’d I tell you?”

“You’re onto something here. I could do this all day.”

She laid back next to me.

“Do you think they’ll be back soon?” I asked.

“It shouldn’t be much longer now.” Rolling onto her side she perched up on her elbow and faced me. “You have came a long way since you ascended, you should be very proud of yourself, I know I am. You know I—never had a sister in my past life. The other Angels are amazing and we’re like family you know?”

"Yeah, it's really something here."

“But when you came here, I *felt* it—this connection with you. You’re the only other Healing Angel to ascend in centuries—I was alone with my gift for so long, I had almost given up the hope of having a sister who shared this profound responsibility.”

Her words meant more than she could have known. “From the moment I met you I wanted to be more like you and you've taught me so much already, you’re the sister I never had, but wish I did.”

"Maybe it's just meant to be the two of us. We have each other that's all we need for our gift."

"You're my sister forever, I want you to know I'm always here for you Jacey." I squeezed her.

"I love you too." We dried our eyes, laughing at our emotional display.

"We're such girls! Now you have me all teary eyed. How am I supposed to train like this?" I motioned to my face, we laughed again.

Zahara hopped up, "The same way *I am!* We're just going to leave the girl talk on the ground here and pick it up later." She waved her hand at the area we were laying, placed her hands on her hips with a nod. "Break time's over, let's go train to kick demon ass!"

"Yes ma'am. Lead the way!" Falling in line behind her as we worked our way through the field.

"So, the life-force guns are self explanatory after the initial test for each Angel. We don't have to waste our time training with them since all we have to do is power it up and-" she made the motion of a small explosion from her chest with her hands. "Boom—what I want to help you with—*are those,"* She pointed to my blades, a wide smile spread across my face.

"You know how to fight with blades too?" Since I'd gotten to know her, I never thought of Zahara as the warrior she looked like.

She carried herself like a skilled fighter, but to me she was more of a comforting healer. “You’re about to find out. Lesson One--” Her sleek sword formed in her hand, the sheen of it reflected in her Jade green eyes. Crouching, she held her blade at an angle and motioned for me to challenge her. “Never let your guard down.”

I readied my Katana, with steady footing, I signaled that I was ready to begin, giving a determined nod. Zahara was stealthy and agile like a cat, but her hits had the force of an NFL linebacker behind them. She wasted no energy with her movements, often my blade missed her by only an inch. When my hits landed, she would take the blows with a laugh and smile.

“I like training with you---” I grunted out as I dipped my body to evade her attack.

“Oh yeah?” She dove at me again, our blades collided, chiming, sending the melody of combat into the air. “Why’s that? I thought you only liked training with *Gideon--”* she teased, mocking my adoration with a whimsical expression as she said the name.

I took advantage of her diverted attention and found my opening. Kicking her body, knocking the wind out of her, my Katana blade rested centimeters away from her neck.

“Never let your guard down.” I sang as we reset our fight.

“Good, fantastic. Lesson number two: Never expect a fair fight.” She looked into the crowd of Warrior Angels, “Kai! Over here!” she yelled. An Angel came out from beside me, I had seen him around at the dinner the night I ascended and also during my brief times training in the field.

He had a rather stocky build, looked to be in his thirties with salt and pepper hair forming at his temples, olive skin, dark hair, and the traditional large vivid blue eyes all the Warrior's shared.

"Kai, this is Jacey, I'm sure you remember. Jacey this is Kai—he's one on *the* best swordsman in the army. *He* is on *my side."*

Terror shook me. *What?! That's not even fair!* Zahara's words resonated in my head. *'Lesson number two: Never expect a fair fight.'* "Ugh!!" I growled, "Why does *everything* have to be so hard?"

"You'll never gain a greater skill if you do not challenge yourself." Kai answered.

He didn't know my question was rhetorical. I assumed what I thought to be a good defensive position, taking out my smaller tanto knife with my free hand. With both blades, I would have a better chance of holding them both at bay and finding an opening for attack. Kai was by my side, Zahara, in front of me an unfair fight wasn't the word, I felt like I was about to be jumped.

CHAPTER THIRTY-EIGHT: CHANGE OF PACE

Defending yourself against a single formidable opponent is challenging, but two opponents was impossible. Kai moved in on my side, each time I would defend an attack from him, Zahara would move in, taking full advantage of the distraction. They beat me again and again.

"Whew!" I panted, Zahara helped me to my feet for the umpteenth time.

"Again!" She pressed.

"I don't know if I'm ready for this."

Kai stood in front of me, his blade in hand, a stone cold look on his face. "One is never ready for the challenges they must face to make them better. In order for you to be ready, you must not have any choice, but to overcome, when failure is no longer an option, at your breaking point, you will find your greatest strength: The heart of a true warrior."

"But I'm not a *warrior*, I am a *Healer* and I've trained a thousand times and I'm still miles behind you both! You've had like a hundred years worth of training!"

Zahara didn't back up, instead she charged and knocked me down, her knee rested on my neck. "When war comes, they will outnumber us a hundred to one. You *must* challenge yourself now, so you may withstand the challenge later."

She took her knee off my throat and stood up, looking down at me as I rubbed my neck. "Do you think we do not know you are at a disadvantage in this war? Your skills are nowhere near the level of ours, that may be true, but you *can* get better, stronger, faster. All you need is a change of pace in your training. Call it a mandatory crash course. *Now get up and fight."*

Standing up, I formulated a new strategy and began utilizing every aspect of my body as a weapon. While I fought Kai with my blades, I would use my legs and wings to hold Zahara at bay, switching back and forth between the two. My senses were in hyper-drive, I could hear them breathing, the humming of their life force. Learning to use my peripheral vision was a challenge I mastered.

We escalated the fights and had to stop to heal the wounds inflicted on each other. One thing was certain: I *was getting better at fighting,* Kai taught me a lot about technique with my blades. How the Tanto was excellent in close quarters combat, the Katana was better for open combat. I could use my sword to keep opponents at bay while being able to deliver lethal blows close range with my knife.

Zahara introduced me to the art of healing while fighting, a difficult task to master, but not impossible. "You cannot expect the fight to stop while you are healing. In this position you and the Angel you are helping are most vulnerable so you must follow the rules." She rushed me while I tried to heal Kai, I defended myself, but she got to Kai before I could counter.

"You see?" she motioned to Kai, "Your comrade would ascend right now." I let out a defeated sigh, shook my head. "No, they would capture him." She gave me a confused look, "Remember?" I explained, "In the vision I had from the Well, Lucifer's army has these cylinders— they were trapping ascending Angels in them, taking them away."

"All the more reason for you to get this right."

It was a challenge throughout the rest of the session, I would defend, attack, practice kill shots, and heal. All the while, failing more often than not. I could no longer complain, their tactics may have been rough, but I was reaping the benefits. There was no denying my improvement. When Gideon and Jesus returned with Maleki and the Watcher Angels, we went to find out what they discovered.

I ran to Gideon, eager to feel the sense of completion from his embrace and pressed my face into his chest. "I missed you."

He kissed my head, "I missed *you."* Jesus and Maleki stood in front of us in the field.

"The Watchers have scanned every access portal into Heaven. They grow weaker as our Father does." hushed whispers swept through the Angels, Jesus clapped his hands. "Shhhh!" He commanded, "Let our brother speak."

Maleki nodded, continuing. "We had reason to believe the attack will take place in Eden. Upon hearing this, we examined the Well of Knowledge and received a powerful vision--" He paused, placing his hand up to quiet everyone down again as everyone shouted questions over one another. The panic in the air was tangible, a blanket of anxiety had covered the field and all of us in it.

"Please, let me finish." Silence fell, "I can say with no uncertainty, that I saw Damien bring the battle to us in Eden. This vision has changed, the battle has changed from what we saw then—to now. The Dark Ones are violent, fierce, and unruly—I saw hundreds of thousands more of them. Their numbers have grown,"

"They send The Dark Ones in the first wave of attack," Maleki continued, "Overwhelming us by shear volume before Damien comes with The Fallen and their beasts. Jesus, Gideon, and I have spent most of the night devising the best method of defense against The Dark Ones. We have worked training to prepare for this war, do not fear this information. As the visions reveal more information, we gain insight and advantage for battle, take comfort in that."

Jesus stepped in front, "We are but days away from the most paramount battle the universe has ever known. You've sacrificed, trained hard, and given it your all—our sister has grown into a skilled fighter. It is thanks to your work, encouragement, and example that this was possible. As a reward for your efforts, I am giving everyone the rest of the day off from training. The leaders and I shall continue working on our countermeasures for the attack. In the meantime, please, take time for yourselves. Enjoy it, for tomorrow, we will no longer be using this field for training, but rather, we will ready for the war in Eden."

The night off sounded like Heaven—but I knew there would be no break for Gideon. He was a leader and therefore, excluded from the luxury of an evening off. That meant no break for me either; a night alone was not something I could attempt until we were certain Lucifer was no longer a threat. I stayed close to Gideon, waiting for the rest of the group leaders to join us. Colin joined us first, he was the fastest and his group fled the moment Jesus dismissed them.

"You're not taking the break? Wow! That's like, *hardcore."* He high-fived me.

"Yeah, It's complicated. I can't be alone yet--" I hesitated, not knowing if all the Angels knew of my relationship to Damien and decided not to elaborate.

He didn't press the subject, just cocked his head a little, then shrugged his shoulders, "Well, that's cool, there's nothin' to do all night at home anyway, this will be more interesting."

"Yes!" Eliza trilled and jumped on my back.

"Hey!" I laughed, flipping her off of me.

"We get to strategize!" She said with a wry smile.

Ashira was the last leader to arrive. Approaching us with a no-nonsense look on her face, she nodded to Jesus. "All right, that's everyone. Let's go guys, we've got work to do." It was time to go back to the last place in Heaven I had ever wanted to go, where it all began, and would end—back to Eden.

CHAPTER THIRTY-NINE: STRATEGY IS KEY

Gideon flew ahead with Maleki and Jesus, leaving us girls in the back with Colin at our side. He was more chatty than the rest of the Angels, his energy was a welcomed breath of fresh air. Hearing him ramble on about possibilities for battle and how we can 'take them' made me smile. I loved his quirky, goofy personality; his innocence was childlike, yet he was mature and capable enough to lead the Messengers.

"So, I was thinking my group should take the first wave. That's what Maleki said they saw right? Waves of attacks?" He continued talking before I could even answer.

"Well, since the messengers are the fastest, it only makes sense for us to be the ones who take out the Dark Ones—since there are so many of them. We can take more of them out with our speed, they won't stand a chance." He shook his fists in excitement and bit his lip, nodding to himself at his idea.

"Let's wait until we get to Eden before we make plans." Ashira said dryly.

"But I—I was just saying--" he stammered. Ashira had the same intimidating effect on everyone. She was older, and wiser, more maternal than the rest of us.

"No 'buts' Colin" She said with disapproval in her tone. "We know nothing yet so please, let us get there first." She nodded to him, waiting for a response.

"Yes, ma'am. Sorry."

Colin's bubble of energy had been popped, and I felt bad for the little guy. But, I could see that like the rest of us, the stress of impending war had taken its toll on Ashira and it had shot her nerves.

It didn't take long before the beautiful sky lost its color, the vibrant landscape was growing darker. We were nearing Eden and my stomach turned when the desolate land came into view. Gideon hung back and flew at my side as we descended.

"Hiya gorgeous." I grinned. "You hanging in there all right?"

"Yup-I'm just ready to get this over with." I sighed. "I feel like we've spent so much time expecting this war, for it to be *here.* It's a little surreal. I mean, we are days away from it now." I shook my head. "It's a scary and unavoidable reality."

"Ah, It'll be over before you know it and we'll be home, together." I smiled at the thought. "Tonight's just about strategy

Love, and that is my specialty." His blue eyes left me breathless, and I scrambled my mind looking for a coherent thought.

"Uh—I know if anyone has a chance at defeating Lucifer, it's us." He wrapped his arm around me, "Atta girl, we'd better get to work then."

We landed in a valley, the dark desolate landscape brought back flashes of the horrors I had witnessed and I shivered, it felt like ice was running through my body. *Get a grip. It's almost over.*

I willed the visions out of my mind as Jesus turned to face us, "We have seen what Lucifer's plans are. We know when Damien will come with his army, and now we know *where.* Gideon, if you would." he gave my hand a little squeeze before walking away.

"All right everybody, listen up. The Dark Ones are coming from the over there." He pointed to the mountains behind him, "Our main goal here is to reinforce the mountains making the chamber more structurally sound. Ashira is it possible with your group?"

Ashira paused, looking behind Gideon at the mountains.

"It's worth a shot and possible. I'm not sure how much that will help with an army that size--" she clicked her tongue and shook her head in thought, "There's no guarantee— that if it were, they won't break through the moment the force field is compromised with a portal."

Gideon nodded. “That's fine, we have to attempt to control the fight as much as possible. They have us beat in numbers, but we have everything else going for us: skill, home field advantage, our new weapon, Intel and strategy. I can work with that and if we all play to our strengths together, victory will be ours.” He bent down and drew in the dirt with a stick.

The two mountains, then the dead river, followed by the surrounding hills. “We must keep them contained to this area between the mountains, no farther than the mouth of the river. If they can spread out, it will be more difficult to fight them and they will slip through, who knows what damage they would do.” He stood up and dusted his hands off.

Eliza spoke, “The Arsenals can create some additional barriers around the designated parameters we can use the same tech from the life-force guns and create a grid to prevent their escape.”

Jesus disagreed, “There is no life-force in Eden. It's a Godforsaken land, Father removed it when he cast Lucifer down and left. There would be nothing to power your barriers so you must think of another way.”

“Well, I guess it's the old fashioned way. Our weapon is sound, if we plan it right, we can divide our groups in waves; half to defend while the others attack. Using your strategy of containing the Dark Ones and Maleki's vision, we will set up individuals from each group to use the life-force guns destroying them as they appear.” She paced holding her finger in the air.

"The others, will pick off the ones that survive. We should switch teams in phases and transition to formal combat when our life-force is too low for us to operate the weapons." She finished with a triumphant nod as we stared at her, shock written on all of our faces. Eliza had came up with an impressive strategy.

"Since there are but two Healers," Zahara said, "We should only divide into two groups, a Healer staying with each one."

Maleki bent down and examined Gideon's drawing, "Let's get a closer look at our battlefield, we can assess the strategy better from there." He looked up at Eliza. "Good job. You have a good plan." She shot a bright smile at him and we walked up the riverbed.

"If they get past us, they'll get to, and destroy Heaven in no time." Jesus said pensively.

"They are fast, and vicious." He continued, "We must do whatever it takes to prevent that from happening. It is imperative they not get to Paradise Valley; it is the only source of God's life-force. If it were compromised— we will never restore the balance."

Zahara rubbed her hand on his back and whispered, "We won't let that happen." He smiled at her holding his hand to her face, I wondered how long they had together as a pair and if I would have the same privilege.

I rested my head on Gideon's shoulder as we walked, memorizing his smell and how he felt. *'You know I love you like crazy woman?'* I smirked.

'How d'you know I could hear you?'

'A little birdie told me... I wasn't sure, so I figured I'd try to see for myself.' I wrapped my arm around his waist. *'Guess you know now. You know I love you like crazy too?'*

He laughed, *'I guess I do now.'*

I bumped him with my hip. *'You 'guess' huh?'* We both giggled playing around bantering back and forth inside our heads until we got there.

Maleki pointed to the crevice between the two adjoining mountains above the hidden cave that led to God's chambers. "This is where they break through— hundreds of thousands." He looked at us all with a sincere concern, "So many—the sky goes black. They blot the light out with Dark Ones."

I looked ahead to the hidden entrance and asked, "What about there? You're certain they don't come from there too?"

"My visions only come in pieces, I could have missed an important detail. So I cannot say for sure."

I looked at Colin, he was still sulking from Ashira snapping at him on our way here. "Colin, do you think your team can handle guarding this entrance and destroying anyone who comes through?"

He looked up thrilled, "We Messengers can handle *anything we'll* eliminate the Dark Ones who try to pass, I guarantee that!"

Jesus flew to the top of the crevice where Maleki said they would come through and we followed. It was a dried up lagoon about a thousand feet wide. When it was Eden, the water was crystal clear with flowering fruit trees and the waterfall roared over the edge hiding God's chambers.

But that was gone now, and the death in its place was a clear reminder of why we were standing here: Lucifer. The mountains on both sides offered plenty of room for groups of Angels to lie in wait. They only lacked cover since the trees were gray twigs sticking up from mangled dried up roots.

"The terrain is rocky" Gideon said as he walked along the area. "It will not be easy to do formal combat here" He looked up at us. "We should take it to the sky, sort our groups and plan around who works best together, strong teams will win this." He looked at Maleki, "How many waves of attack did you see?"

Maleki's eyes went blank as he recalled his premonition. "I see two. The Dark Ones come first. Then *they come* The Fallen and the Beasts." I felt the familiar pang of fear shoot through me, again doubting my ability to fight in this war.

But I couldn't let that spook me, not now. Not after all the hard work I had put into training. Even if I had trained for a hundred years, I doubt I would ever feel 'ready.' maybe everyone shared the same fear as me, and they didn't show it.

"We should focus on groups of fifty or less for now, unless we get more information in the next few days." Gideon said. "We need to make sure there are enough of us to cycle out between the waves of attack. If we train with this strategy here in mind, I know we will defeat Lucifer. We may not destroy his army, but we can force them to retreat, and that's a win."

Jesus looked around to us. "We have a good plan, we're done, thank you all for your help. I would like time alone now if you don't mind. I'll see everyone tomorrow." We said our goodbyes and left as Zahara stayed behind with Jesus.

"Do you think Jesus is okay?" I asked Gideon as we flew. "I mean, he seemed so... *sad* just now. Do you think he fears we will lose?"

"Well, I think we *all* fear we will lose Love. What Jesus fears most is for our Father's safety, and the safety of others. I think no one in his position would be 'okay' there's a lot riding on his shoulders here."

He looked off into the distance and spoke, almost to himself, "He's questioning whether he did enough. If he is good enough of a leader to pull this off. He's wondering how many of us he'll lose, and how he'll deal with the pain of those losses. But if anyone can handle all of that, Jesus can. I promise, Love."

CHAPTER FORTY: GIDEON'S SERENADE

"I promised myself I would take care of something as soon as we made up before you left and went with Jesus to find The Watchers." I said to Gideon. We were still on our way home from Eden and the sky was losing its dead and dreary gray color, returning to its bright and colorful glory as we entered Heaven.

"Oh? And what would that be Love?"

"I want to know where you live."

Gideon snickered, "Wow, that was easy. I'm surprised you came right out with it rather than argue with yourself for fifteen minutes before you settle on saying what's on your mind."

"I *do not!"* I scoffed.

"Okay, whatever you say, Love. Just know, I've been in there with you." He pointed to my head, I pushed him.

"I'm an analytical person, I like to make sure of what I'm saying before committing to saying it that's all."

"Follow me, you only get to see it *if* you can keep up." He sped ahead of me, leaving me in his proverbial Angel dust. "Oh no you don't!" I yelled out, pumping my wings in full force to generate enough speed to catch him. "Come on slowpoke you have better than that in you don't you?" He teased hollering over his shoulder.

Oh Gideon McGrath if you weren't already dead I could kill you for making me chase you like this! I pushed myself farther across the sky willing my wings to move faster until I felt I couldn't move them anymore than what I already had and caught up to him.

A mountainside with the fire-like colors of a New England fall was beneath us. The giant trees had a rich abundance of orange, red, yellow and green leaves. Gideon descended and looked up watching as I landed next to him.

"Come on, follow me." He walked up a tiny trail into the woods and I followed. With no house in sight after a twenty minute hike I couldn't help but wonder how far Gideon really lived in these mountains.

"Why do you live so deep in the woods?"

We approached a small creek with a wooden bridge and crossed it. "I like my privacy. The woods always gave me a sense of peace and serenity. I'm comfortable here." A house came into view, "Wow." I breathed. It looked like a picture from town and country magazine rustic and charming. There was a rock mosaic walkway that forked off; one path led to a garden, the other to his stairs.

Gideon's home was a gorgeous cabin made of rough cut lumber, as if he had built it with his own two hands. It had green shudders and a tin roof. The porch had a banister composed of knotty branches, they were smooth and treated, placed to give it an artistic touch. A wooden porch swing hung at the end, and a small round stump table with a rocking chair sat beside it.

"Gideon, it's—beautiful."

He started up the steps, extended his hand, and we went inside. Inside, it was small and simple but there was character and thoughtfulness everywhere I looked. Bookshelves lined his walls filled with hundreds of old books from classic authors such as Hemingway, Dickens and Edgar Allan Poe. His home was cozy and practical, nothing extra it was just the necessities. I walked through the rooms, taking my time, feeling like I could see a different side of Gideon.

There was a lot of green throughout the house, I noticed. From the curtains, blankets, towels, and rugs, the bright signature Irish color adorned every room. He looked vulnerable and nervous watching me examine his home. "Do you like it?"

"Of course I do, It's you... down to the last detail, perfect." His lips parted in a grin. "I'm glad you approve it, Love." He grabbed my wrist and pulled me towards him, we swayed back and forth, slow dancing to our own silent song. The song that plays in your heart that only your soulmate can sing to you, and boy did Gideon know how to sing to mine.

He spun me around and dipped me, supporting me in his strong, stable arms and held me down with his lips pressed against mine. These were the rare occurrences of private intimacy I cherished. "You're my everything, woman." He whispered, as we continued dancing, my head resting on his chest. Lost in the rhythm of his words, I closed my eyes as he spoke, a beautiful serenade.

"Oh, call it by some better name. For friendship sounds too cold. While love is now a worldly flame, Whose shrine must be of Gold: And passion, like the sun at noon, That burns o'er all he sees. A while as warm will set as soon—Then call it none of these. Imagine something purer far, more free from stain of clay. Then friendship, Love, or Passion are, Yet human still as they: And if thy lip, for love like this, No mortal word can frame, Go ask the Angels what it is, And call it by that name."

We had stopped moving, time hadn't caught up yet to where we were and I prayed it never would; that we could live forever in this moment.

"My mother used to read poetry at night to help me fall asleep. This was one of her favorite writers, Thomas Moore. I never understood those words, before you, my heart didn't know the depths of such things. But, after I ascended when you became my charge, I looked after you, and fell in love with you, before we'd even spoken a word. Then that poem was in my heart for you, and I knew."

"Knew what?"

"I knew we paired together, you were mine and I've never been happier, never felt more complete."

We rested our foreheads against each other's. There were no more words left to say; we had everything between us. Even in the face of a situation as dire as Armageddon, we could escape, retreating into a love that made my fear disappear. I ran my fingers through his hair, playing with his wild curls. He walked over to the couch, pulling me by the hand.

"Come here you,--let me hold you for a while." I laid next to him, our bodies molding together, his arms wrapped around me in contentment. "Gideon?" I looked up at him, "Yes?"

"I want to know more about you. I feel you know everything about me already. Can you tell me about your life? Where were you born? What are your favorite things? I want to know everything."

He laughed and kissed my temple. "Eh, I'll put you to sleep with all that." he joked. "Okay, where shall I begin? Well, I was born in Ireland, the year was 1896, in a little village called Brookeborough. My father was a sheep farmer, I had two younger brothers, Ian and Liam. My dad taught me about farming, my mother schooled me and my brothers. When I was old enough, I worked for myself and saved enough money to buy land of my own." He paused and looked uncomfortable, I knew it was about Mary. "Go ahead," I said, urging him to continue.

"Well, um, then I met Mary when I was leaving the local pub one night, we were young and I fell for her. She was kind and sweet with stubbornness to her, like someone else I know." I grinned, thinking about her beautiful face, so full of love and life in our shared memory. "Well, you saw the rest; it wasn't soon after we wed that I enlisted in the war, there isn't much more after that."

"Well, what are your favorite things? What were your parents names?"

He laughed at my insistence. "I like making things and growing them, working with my hands always gave me a sense of accomplishment, I love writing and reading not that there was anything else to do. You know the world I was born into didn't offer much. Oh, but I could get lost in books, they will always be around to stand the test of time." I was glad he was also an avid reader. "My moms name is Catherine, and my dad's is Connor." He sighed, "There isn't anything else Love. My life was rather uneventful, and like yours, cut short."

"That's fine, I feel like I know more about your life as a human. That's all I wanted." I kissed his cheek and rolled into face him.

"You always are." He let me nestle in, resting his chin on my head. Our legs wrapped around one another's; we laid in a tangled knot on the couch.

I drifted off to sleep, too comfortable to fight the urge to stay awake. Or maybe I wanted to let go of all the stress for a while, I don't know. But when I awoke, Gideon was gone. A sharp sense of dread ran through me and I jumped up calling for him.

"Gideon?! Where are you?" A clatter came from the kitchen, I followed the noise to find him donning an apron over the small stove.

"Hey there's my sleeping beauty! Did you have a good rest love? I thought I'd surprise you and fix you some breakfast before we head out."

Breakfast? Before we head out? It confused me, "How long did I sleep for? It's time to go back already?"

"Not long, we only had a couple hours anyway, you needed to rest, and *I* needed to show off my cooking skills… Coffee?" He handed me a mug.

"Thank you." I took a sip, the familiar taste brought me back to my life as a med student. The long hours of studying and endless work resulted in lack of sleep. I lived on coffee and energy drinks during finals.

Gideon sat down with our plates, he had made omelettes with a side of fresh berries. "It looks delicious." I said, grabbing my fork and taking a bite and swallowed, "You definitely have skills worth showing off." Eating gave me a strange sensation in my stomach; there was no relief from hunger and it felt unusual. It still tasted good, the omelettes were fluffy and filled with cheese and veggies, topped with chives and salted to perfection.

"Thank you. I racked my brain trying to think of what you'd like, and then I figured, who doesn't like a good omelette?" We finished our breakfast, and I helped clean up, feeling him wrap his arms around my waist from behind me and kiss my shoulder. I'd dreamed of a relationship like this in the past and played out this exact moment in my mind a thousand times wishing for God to send me the right man to share it with.

"You know I love you so much right?" He squeezed me, turning me into face him, "I do, and I promise when this was is over, and we no longer have to look over our shoulders, I will steal you away for a while, keep you all to myself." he kissed my nose. "Speaking of which—we'd better get going, I'm sure the others are there already."

"I guess this will be the last chance we get to spend together until this is over." The anxiety of the war weighed heavy in my words. He caressed my cheek with the back of his hand, "I'm counting down the moments love. This'll all be over before you know it. There's nothing to worry about okay? You will be fine, I'll make sure if it."

But it wasn't me, it was everyone's lives and everything that still hung in the balance. I had to get my head right worrying want going to help us defeat Lucifer's army. "I know you will. We'll all look out for each other, we'd better get going." He gave my shoulders a squeeze and rubbed my arms.

"Yeah love, it's time."

We headed back to Eden, I said a little prayer to our father to be with us, we would need it.

CHAPTER FORTY-ONE: THE FINAL COUNTDOWN

Approaching Eden filled me with an impending sense of dread as if I could already feel the darkness of Lucifer. Gideon sensed my unease and tried to reassure me. "You know, we have some of the greatest minds and gifts that God has ever created Love." He tilted his head to meet my eyes, "I will stay right by your side, we will work together, follow the strategy and send them back to Hell. Believe Love." His eyes twinkled, hopeful.

"I know," I parted my lips, "It all happened so fast, I—can't believe it's already here you know? Like, I knew from the moment I got here that this would happen but somehow, it still feels like it wasn't enough time." I let out a slow breath. "We can do this, I am certain if it. But the *fear...* It's still in there too, no matter how hard I try to fight it, *it's still there.*"

He held my hand, "Then *use it* to your advantage. Think about whatever fears you have, and plan for them, face them."

I saw our glorious Army when we landed and a shocked breath escaped me. Each group of Angels appeared war ready; in full fighting gear and looking fierce. A weight lifted from me, I could breathe a little easier. *Look at them. They're ready, we all are.* My life-force surged through me like a shot of adrenaline to my heart. Gideon felt my confidence, "That's my girl."

We approached the base of the river and fell in line next to Jesus and the leaders. He was planning the specifications of our strategy; choosing who would be in each group and when they were to cycle out.

"There will be fifty-one in each group. Composed of teams of ten from each group and one Healer. This is not including the Messengers; they will guard alternate exits and warning us of any further breaches made by the Dark Ones."

He turned and motioned towards the areas we had selected for the groups to lie in wait. "The first and second group has to be our strongest and most experienced fighters. The Dark Ones are coming with numbers never seen and we must focus on eliminating them *before* they swarm us."

He jumped up to the top the mountains, standing on the right side, to better explain. "We will have a clear vantage point from here, and there when they break through. If The Watchers visions are correct, which I'm sure they are, we can expect a flood of Dark Ones in the middle here. While the first two groups are attacking the initial wave of Dark Ones, the rest of us will take the fight to the sky." He paused as the Angels talked amongst each other, and cleared his throat, speaking louder.

"Brothers, sisters, we have no room for error here, so listen! We must contain their army and keep the fight here in Eden. Even a *single* Dark One can lay waste to thousands and wreak havoc in Paradise Valley. *We must* protect the innocents at all costs!" He took a deep breath, our army stood clinging to his words. I could hear his desperation breaking through his voice and knew Jesus was feeling the enormity of the clock ticking, counting down the seconds to our attack.

The tension was thick in the air around Eden, and deep down, we were all terrified. "We decided that we will use our life-force guns, as you all know, we cannot afford to fire them recklessly; not without draining too much energy from us. Hence the reason we divide into groups.

"The point is to fire your weapon at the point of maximum damage—wait until you can take out *many* Dark Ones, not just one. If you encounter a straggler, use your training and traditional combat to destroy it and do not waste your life-force. The Healers will be the only Angels in the active attack at all times, the rest of us will cycle out to recharge our life-force. I ask each of you to take on the additional responsibility to *protect* your Healers.

"Make sure you all stay alert. We have less than three days to train and devise a workable strategy, questions anyone?" He asked, but the crowd was mute. "Good, divide into your groups and await further instruction from your leader. We've got much to do, with many training drills over the next couple of days. Let's waste no time." The Angels broke off and Jesus turned back to face us.

"I've been giving much thought to everything and I think we should assume that each group will have to eliminate ten thousand Dark Ones before they cycle out." Gideon blew out a large breath and ran his hand over his head. "Wow---ah, that's a lot." Jesus placed a hand on Gideon's shoulder and raised his eyebrows, "We knew they would outnumber us—This is the reality of the situation."

"With the right plan, we can win sir."

Ashira stepped forward and touched Jesus' shoulder. "I believe the Elementals can help funnel them, I've been running a plan through my mind that may work to our advantage."

Jesus' face grew intrigued. "What did you have in mind?"

She pointed to the area before the dried up lagoon, "There. It's wide open if it stays that way they have the chance to get by and spread." She lifted her hand, and the ground shook, like an earthquake was hitting. The low rumble echoed through the valley with a thunderous roar and the Earth rose forming high walls between the ridges. She turned to face us.

"The Elementals can build another mountain here, connecting the other two to it so we can block them in as they come out controlling their staggering numbers."

"Wonderful! Yes, do whatever you feel will help us, but do it so we can train with it!"

Ashira signaled down to her group and brought them up behind us, putting them to work creating a fortress of mountains around us.

Gideon leaned over and whispered in my ear, "I better get going, Love. I've got leading to do, be back before ya know it." He kissed my cheek and flew down to his Warrior's his sword in the air yelling and pumping them up.

Eliza took a wide step next to me, nudging me with a smile. "How are you holding up?" I didn't understand how she could have such an optimistic brightness to her, even in the face of destruction. "Um... Good—I'm doing good. Nervous, but good. I've never feared something yet wanted it to happen this bad all at the same time before so---that's new." She laughed out loud and covered her mouth with her hands, then reached to hug me.

"I know what you mean. But we must believe we will *win this."* She looked at me, "There is no other way for life to go on. We must win because failing, isn't an option for anyone." I smiled grunting as she squeezed me super hard in a bear hug. "I've got to go get my troops." She saluted me and walked backwards, bumping into Ashira then fervently apologizing, making me laugh as Zahara joined me.

"Time to assemble the Healing Angels." she said and then looked around, "Well, looks like we're all here." I was still laughing.

"Oh Zahara," I shook my head. "What are we going to do?" She wrapped her arm around my shoulder, guiding me up the mountainside. "*We* will wait for the leaders to divide their groups and rest while they do it."

I gave her my best 'are you crazy?' look, and she placed her finger in the air, "I know what you're thinking but let me explain. We will be so busy fighting and healing non-stop when the time comes—*we need this rest."* She stopped and turned to face me, "Trust me, Jacey. We do."

I could not argue, she had made a valid, logical decision, and she was my leader. We would sit and rest while the others figured everything else out. For now, they already set our roles in stone; we were to heal the thousands of Angels that would need it when the time came. I never imagined how fast that day would come.

Between dividing the groups and running drills, the next two days flew by in the blink of an eye. We worked hard, trying to strategize and plan for every possible scenario, and when the night of the eclipse came, we laid in wait for their attack.

CHAPTER FORTY-TWO: THE DARK ONES

Gideon held my hand, he hadn't left my side since we assumed formation. We waited, and I stared at the ground in front of us afraid to blink. My eyes burned, but I couldn't bring myself to look away, even for a second.

Half of me expected them to burst through bringing this dreaded war to life while the other half still held hope for a miracle. I'd prayed that maybe, just maybe, they wouldn't be able to create the portal, and that they could spare us from this war.

But the hope I had clung to was lost when a crash shook the mountains. *It's starting. Oh God, help us.* “Be ready!” Gideon shouted, I looked at him with trepidation, “I love you.” he said, I hugged him tightly. “I love you too, I always will.” I whispered, turning back to face what was to come.

“Remember your training!” Jesus called down from above us as the ground shattered, gaping open, and that dreaded moment came to be. Dark Ones exploded out with the force of an oil strike shooting into the air, filling the sky until all you could see, was them.

They came in droves of thousands, scrambling over each other lusting for the fight. Each face, twisted and mangled, with hollowed eyes and razor sharp jagged teeth dripping with venom. They were closing in on us from every angle, with more flooding out as each second passed.

"Hold!" Jesus yelled. Time stopped, as if the entire scene was playing out in slow motion before my eyes. Each agonizingly long second drug into the next taking all of my energy to fight the fear that threatened to consume me. I wanted to run, terrified that there were just too many. *Will this be the end of us?*

I looked around at our group everyone was staring at the portal watching the massive army grow larger. Each Angel held the same determined look on their face, but the fear I felt, was also in their eyes. Gideon froze, looking up, waiting for Jesus to make his move.

"Charge your weapons!" He ordered. The mountains lit up with the blue glow of our life-force guns. We held the charge, row by row. "Now! First attackers, aim for the portal, the second wave, take the flanks!" Jesus barked over the shrieks of the Dark Ones.

When the first round fired, it obliterated the Dark Ones, they vanished in a cloud of dust as their own black life-force escaped them. By the time the second wave hit, they had evaded the beams with the speed and agility of a cheetah. *They're too fast!* Screams filled the air from the Angels who were being injured, and

I rushed to their aid, healing as fast as I could. We continued fighting for our lives as more attacked.

They were horrifying to look at, gargoyle like creatures with slimy gray skin and bat-like wings. But that wasn't even the worst part, the worst part was how violent, fast and strong they were. Like rabid dogs, they snapped their jaws at me and swung their massive claws, knocking me onto my back, tearing at my armor.

I made fast work with my blades using every bit of my training to counter with kill shots. With my Katana, I could behead them with a single slice. Then I used my tanto to slice open their chests, releasing their life-force. They were ravenous looking demons, trained and created with the sole purpose of killing us.

My eyes shot around as thousands more made their ascent from the portal, I couldn't see Gideon anywhere. "Gideon!" I screamed. "Gideon!" but my voice was drowned out by the sound of the battle. I could see Angels who needed me strewn across the mountainside writhing in agony from the venom. *They're ascending, NO!*

I flew, jumped, climbed and ran all over healing without so much as a wasted second, but I still couldn't get to everyone. We were losing precious lives, and I cried, mourning the loss, feeling my failure. I watched, as I made it to some in time, and came too late for others.

We cycled out the groups, and the war waged on for hours. There was still no sign of Gideon. All I could do was fulfill my duty and pray that he was somewhere safe. Jesus and the others were high above us, ensuring no Dark One escaped by flight from Eden. I killed hundreds, maybe thousands and healed everyone I could find. We pressed on until we had eliminated every Dark One, and the portal fell still in the night.

CHAPTER FORTY-THREE: THE FALLEN

Unable to afford to let our guard down, we assumed formation and my heart sang in sweet relief as I saw my love. "I was looking everywhere for you! You had me so worried!"

"Sorry, Love but I was fine!" His face grew serious, and he motioned towards the portal. "Time to focus, be ready."

It glowed like liquid magma was swirling inside a tunnel of flames, we held our positions and charged our life-force guns, waiting. The Fallen were coming any minute and would be bringing the Beasts with them. They shot up from the portal like rockets, moving so fast they were a dark blur in the sky. They looked like Angels clothed in black and red battle attire, and their stripped wings were painfully gruesome to look at.

Three of them dove at Jesus, pushing him out of the safety of his group and surrounded him, leaving no chance of a clear shot. Jesus was a mighty warrior though, bigger and stronger than The Fallen, and he looked like he had the situation under control; with magnificent sword work and instantaneous reflexes. He countered every attack with the speed and precision of a vetted warrior of God.

More Fallen came through bringing the Beasts out, my mouth gaped at the sight. They looked like giant failed science experiments animalistic vicious Demons a hundred times our size, they leapt up the mountains in a single bound. We fired, one, two, three times, but they did not falter. Shaking off the sting of our beams like a mosquito.

"What do we do?" I yelled to Gideon, he didn't look phased and smiled with excitement. "We do this the old fashioned way Love." He winked at me and jumped down the cliff, landing in front of the beast. "Hey! Oh you're an ugly bastard ain't ya?" He taunted, twirling his sword. "let me fix your face for ya!" It lunged at him and I covered my mouth holding in a scream.

He jumped up, escaping its snapping jaws, flying behind it, then underneath, confusing the creature as it whirled around trying to devour him. He landed on its back, thrusting his sword down into its neck. A wretched howl escaped from it as he pulled down on his sword dragging it around in a circle until the head of the beast rolled off onto the ground.

I wanted to vomit and congratulate him at the same time for his impressive skills but I had work to do. More beasts had made their way through the portal and Angels were falling from the sky at the hands of The Fallen. The skill they possessed matched ours, and their weapons included fantastic swords, and venom, I guess they had figured that would be enough.

While I was assisting a wounded warrior, one of them snuck up on me, kicking me back and drive his sword into my comrade. "Noooooo!" I screamed as I witnessed the life-force leave him. The Fallen Angel pulled out a familiar cylinder, sucking up the warrior's life-force, trapping him and preventing his rightful ascension.

I screamed and dove at him, fighting for my fallen friends. "You're gonna pay for that!" I growled through my teeth.

He gave me a wicked grin, his black eyes gleaming, "You cannot win this... *Child."* He taunted as I lunged forward slicing at him with my blades. Our skills were matched equally; his reflexes just as fast as mine, every hit was countered, but I would not give up and pressed on.

He swung his sword, and I tucked down, and wounded him sliding through his legs, cutting him on his thigh. I stood up crossing my blades like scissors, his head rolled down and his body fell limply to its knees. "Told you, you'd pay for that." I said, picking up the cylinder before opening his chest.

The screams for help were deafening me, I stood up with a heavy breath, winded from the fight. I was exhausted, and my life-force was depleted but everywhere I looked Angels needed my help. I could barely fly and healing was taking longer, but I healed many.

We came together and fought. Though we'd suffered losses, the tides turned in our favor and the last of The Fallen was finally eliminated with his beast. Something wasn't right; I hadn't seen Damien anywhere, and I had a bad feeling.

CHAPTER FORTY-FOUR: THE GUARDIANS

We came together at the base of the mountain cheering in victory. I didn't want to spoil the mood ranting about my suspicions and joined in the merriment. All the leaders remained, even Colin, and the Messengers flew up when they heard our celebration.

It flooded me with relief at the sight of the young Messengers; we spared them from the true horror of this war and I couldn't have been happier. It seemed all was well, like we had succeeded in our quest to defend heaven and then I saw him.

He was there in an instant, no fancy show, no movement from the portal, no ground shaking. Damien had just *appeared, and he wasn't alone.* My eyes widened, and everyone turned to see them. *Oh my God... It's them.*

The Guardians I saw when I visited God, were of a pure white life-force, but these Guardians were not. They were a dark energy of black and purple, wore black robes, and wielded the swords of Lucifer with Damien, Evil was their master, they were The Guardians of Hell now.

As they filled the area, surrounding us appearing to materialize from thin air Jesus hissed, “Charge your weapons and fire as soon as you can!” Without hesitation, we lit up the lagoon and firing all we had.

That was the last thing I remembered when I opened my eyes. The shot had drained me, I'd used too much of my life-force and now laid helpless on the ground as the other Angels fought around me in a blur.

“Jacey! Get up Love. You've got to get up—Jacey!” Gideon shouted looking down at me.

He was holding a Guardian at bay with his sword, gritting his teeth, he pushed it back, taking the fight away from me. I breathed hard, willing myself to be stronger, to get up and fight. As soon as I stood up, I got knocked down by a massive blow to my chest. A whimper came up my throat as I contemplated my demise.

Oh my God. This is the end of me. A Guardian loomed over me, his sword in hand and all I could do was close my eyes. *I love you Gideon, I'm sorry.* A loud scream came, and I opened my eyes to see Gideon plunging his sword through my attacker.

He pushed the body aside, dropping to his knees to lift me up. “It's okay Love, I'm here. I got you.” he said, lifting me into his arms with ease. His blue eyes shimmered as he smiled down at me that's when I heard it; the unforgettable, terrible sound and the soft agony filled grunt that escaped Gideon as I slipped from his hands, his face froze.

"GIDEON? NOOOOOO!" I screamed in anguish, tears flooded my eyes blurring my vision but not to where I couldn't see: It was *him.* Damien stood with a wry smile behind Gideon, holding the sword that protruded from his chest. I died in that instant.

"I wanted you—but this one will just have to do I guess—*if* he makes it that is." He cocked his head to look at Gideon, Laughing as my love writhed from the burning venom. "Looks like I gotta go sis, gotta get him *home*." He smiled a sinister smile, "Come visit anytime, I'm sure a long distance relationship wasn't part of your plan but well, you know—things change." His face grew serious with his final taunt, "You want him? Come and get him." He pulled Gideon back, disappearing into thin air as I screamed. "Gideon!!! Bring him back!!! Gideon!!! Oh my God!" I was inconsolable.

The Guardians vanished back to Hell. Jesus, and the others surrounded me. Eliza and Zahara picked me up, mourning for my loss hurt me. The pain from losing Gideon was worse than anything I had ever experienced. Worse than my death, this was just—unbearable.

I dried my tears and turned to face Jesus. "We need to find Gideon and bring him back! I will not leave him down there! I *will* save him with or without you!" Jesus' eyes were hazy, he lifted his hands, holding my shoulders. "Jacey, you can barely stand--"

"I DON'T CARE! I'm not leaving him!!"

He shushed me. "I understand, okay? But *you* will not go to get Gideon--" his words crushed my heart, I looked at him in disbelief, "We all are*."* I collapsed into his arms, sobbing. "Thank you! Thank you Jesus!"

He looked around at the leaders, even beaten down and exhausted each of them was still willing to fight for Gideon. "We need another plan."

'Just hang on Gideon' I thought, praying to God that somehow he would hear me, even in Hell. '*We're coming my love. Just hang on.'*

The Angel Chronicles

Lucifer's Wrath

J.L. Rodriguez

Made in the USA
Columbia, SC
04 December 2024